M000205906

I Hear the Human Noise

I Hear the
Human
Noise

Stories by

Ray Morrison

Press 53
Winston-Salem

Press 53, LLC
PO Box 30314
Winston-Salem, NC 27130

First Edition

Copyright © 2019 by Ray Morrison

All rights reserved, including the right of reproduction in
whole or in part in any form except in the case of brief quotations
embodied in critical articles or reviews. For permission, contact
publisher at Editor@Press53.com, or at the address above.

Cover design by Claire V. Foxx
and Kevin Morgan Watson

Cover art, "Static Waveform," Copyright © 2009 by Mark Ross,
licensed through iStock

Library of Congress Control Number
2019936491

This is a work of fiction. Names, characters, places, and incidents
are products of the author's imagination or are used fictionally.
Any resemblance to actual events, locales, or persons,
living or dead, is entirely coincidental.

Printed on acid-free paper
ISBN 978-1-950413-06-5

For my siblings,
both in blood and marriage,
great friends all.

Grateful acknowledgment is made to the editors of the following publications in which these stories first appeared:

2 *Bridges Review*, "Secret Santa Gift" (published as "Secret Santa")

Beloit Fiction Journal, "Dawn Branch"

The Broad River Review, "Custody Battle" and "No One's Ghost but My Own"

Don't Talk to Me about Love, "Fire and Ice"

Fiction Southeast, "Swing"

Isthmus, "For You"

Kestrel, "Ripples"

Sand Hills Magazine, "Return to Harmony"

Short Story America, Volume V, "The Projectionist's Daughter" (published in a slightly different form as "Doyle's Diner")

storySouth, "What Courage Looks Like"

Contents

I could hear my heart beating. I could hear everyone's heart. I could hear the human noise we sat there making, not one of us moving, not even when the room went dark.

—Raymond Carver,
"What We Talk About When We Talk About Love"

Dawn Branch

Ma'am, I need you to calm down so I can help you."
The 911 operator sits up. On the other end of the
line the woman's voice is shrill, nearly incoherent. The
dispatcher surmises enough from the panicked words to
understand the woman's daughter has fallen into the river
and is in trouble. The operator asks the woman's location,
already tapping buttons on her computer to summon the
rescue squad and sheriff as she tries to pinpoint the call
with GPS. The mother wails from the other end of the line,
and the operator presses her again for a specific location
or landmark to aid the first responders in getting to her
quickly. The mother calms down enough to give a few
clues—a sharp bend in the river, a truck repair shop close
to where they turned off the main road, a small clearing
by the water where they set up their picnic—but they are
enough for the dispatcher, a local woman who has spent
her entire life in these North Carolina mountains, to figure
out the woman is near the wide, deep bend of the Pigeon
River close to the Dawn Branch. The operator alerts the
rescue squad out of Crabtree. She then tells the mother

that help is fifteen minutes away, to stay on the line, and to tell her when she hears the sirens. The mother is sobbing and no longer speaks.

When the rescue squad arrives at the scene, they find a woman and a man standing near the water. The man's hair and clothes are soaked and he is shivering violently. One of the two rescue squad members hurries to the back of their vehicle and retrieves a heavy blanket to wrap around the man. The woman grabs the other EMT, a part-time volunteer in his mid-twenties who owns a bait and tackle shop in town, and pulls him by his wrist to the water's edge. She points downstream, explaining that their daughter waded into the river and was quickly pulled away. The rescuer stares at the surging water. It has rained hard for most of the previous week, so the water level is high and the current dangerous. He hesitates to look the woman in the eyes.

The men from the rescue squad confer quietly by their truck. The girl has most likely drowned, but her body needs to be found. The older one, another part-timer who has fished in this river for over forty years and knows just how treacherous these waters can be, wonders how many days will pass before the river decides to send the girl back—if ever. He unclips his radio and calls for additional help. They'll need equipment and a diver, maybe a helicopter from Asheville. He checks his watch. They have two or three hours at most before daylight fades.

The sheriff arrives and leads the mother and father back up the bank to the dirt road, where his car is parked. Blue lights flash from atop the vehicle, bright even in the daylight, causing the woman to squint. The sheriff leans through the window and shuts off the lights. The mother is no longer hysterical but appears to the sheriff to be on the verge of collapsing. The father, who has not spoken, grasps the EMS blanket tight around him, his mouth drooping open, his eyes red and moist. When the sheriff asks them to describe what happened, his voice is nearly a whisper. The sheriff has dealt once before with a dead child—the victim of a car wreck—and he knows he must not push too hard right now.

The mother stares at the ground and begins to tell what happened. They'd moved earlier this summer from down on the coast to a new home in Winston-Salem. Their daughter had not adjusted well. Their house had been gloomy and the recent week of nonstop rain had not helped. When this morning brought sunshine and clear skies, she and her husband came up with the idea to take a trip to the mountains to have a picnic.

The sheriff glances down toward the riverbank at the crumpled blanket with plastic containers of half-eaten potato salad and fried chicken. Near one edge of the blanket is an iPhone in a bright pink case. He writes in a small notebook.

The daughter, who'd just turned twelve, seemed to have come out of her funk, appearing happy for the first time in a long while, the mother explains. After lunch, however, the girl said she wanted to take a walk in the woods.

"We begged her to wait for us but she pouted and said she was not a baby. . .she was old enough to go alone. We told her to be careful and stay far away from the water. Ten minutes later, we heard her screaming. We jumped up, only to see her float past right there," the woman points at the river just beyond the picnic site, "struggling to keep her head above water. But the water was rushing so fast that she was nearly out of sight before we could move. We ran along the edge of the water, but it was hard to keep up. Her head kept disappearing below the surface, each time for longer and longer. That final time, when she didn't come back up at all, my husband ran into the river but was knocked down by the rapids, which pulled him under too. He was just able to scramble back to the shore, but we never saw our daughter again."

The sheriff stops writing and places the notebook back into his shirt pocket. He signals to the rescuer down by the water—the other has already started searching the bank downstream—and asks the man and woman to take the EMT to the spot where they last saw their daughter. More sirens begin to sound in the distance. The sheriff waits for the additional help while the parents lead the young man from the rescue squad down the bank.

Thirty minutes later, the girl's parents sit in the backseat of the sheriff's cruiser and wait. They cling to each other, motionless. There are nine searchers now, and the sheriff stands on the muddy bank next to the river, smoking a cigarette and listening on his radio for any progress. The ground here is slick, and the mud has a silver-brown shine. He watches a school of minnows glide past close to the water's edge. When his radio crackles, he jumps. His dispatcher tells him that the diver is ten minutes out. The sheriff looks across the river, to the west. Rust-colored streaks begin to appear in the sky. He goes back to the car to update the girl's parents and to wait for the diver.

As the sheriff starts up the hill, there's a sudden squall of voices on his radio. The girl's body has been found. The sheriff asks if he should send the diver home. A voice he doesn't recognize tells him that she is trapped between two large rocks. The diver will need to go in for her.

The diver is a man in his thirties, a zoology professor at Warren Wilson College, who also teaches scuba diving at the YMCA. The professor climbs into his wet suit behind his truck while the sheriff updates him. Over his shoulders the diver slings an air tank and a backpack filled with coils of rope. Walking down to the river, he glances into the sheriff's car at the grieving parents, who stare at him as he passes by. The diver looks away quickly. Members of the search team begin to lead the diver to the spot where the girl was found. The sheriff takes a deep breath and walks to his car to inform the mother and father. Even before he reaches the cruiser he can see in their eyes that they already know.

As the diver approaches the site, a group of men and women with grim expressions stand silently. He turns to the river and, right away, spots the body. Only one of the girl's legs is visible, wedged between two large rocks about twenty feet from the riverbank. Her bare foot floats on the surface, swaying back and forth with the roiling current, as if she is dancing to an unheard song. The diver dips his mask in the water and secures two ropes around his waist—one for the girl, one for himself should he get into trouble.

The girl is lying on her back, bobbing under the water like one of the preserved animal specimens the diver has in his lab back at the college, and in the dim light and murky water, her form has an indistinct and ghostly appearance. The diver can see clearly enough that her eyes and mouth are wide open, yet he can't tell if it was surprise or wonder that filled her final moments. The girl's tee shirt is torn and bunched at her armpits by the rough water. She is wearing a training bra, one side of which has been pulled away. It's the sight of the girl's budding breast that will haunt the diver on many nights, keeping him awake for years to come. He is battered by the swirling current but manages to tie one of the ropes from his waist around her ankle before pulling the girl's leg free from where it became stuck in the rocks. He jerks the line three times, and from under the water, he watches the girl glide away, released from the river that tried to claim her forever.

Before leaving the river, the diver stares down into the blackness beneath the rocks and the raging river, imagining the girl's soul there, stuck in the turbulent silt at the bottom until the end of days.

The woman is awakened by a bright light. She squints at the shaft of sunlight slipping through the bedroom window's partially closed blinds. The light is momentarily disorienting. *At last*, she thinks, *the rain has stopped. Another bleak day inside this house would be too much.* She twists to look at her husband, who is still asleep, his back to her. The woman slips her legs off the side of the bed and sits up, stretching. Her first thought is to make coffee, but as she stands, she remembers the fight from the night before, and her good mood disappears. It was a bad one.

The woman pees and then brushes her teeth before pushing the chair blocking their bedroom door back to its customary place and heading downstairs to start the coffeemaker. At the top of the stairs, she glances at the closed door of her daughter's room. She tries hard not to recall the ugly things that were done and said last night, but the effort only brings the memories faster. Most anguishing is remembering the conversation she had later, in bed, with her husband. The woman bites her lip hard and descends the stairs.

Their house is old, built in the first decade of the twentieth century, and the windows on the main floor are tall and wide, filling the house with early morning light. The woman walks into the kitchen and methodically begins to grind beans and fill the coffeemaker with water. While she waits for the coffee to brew, she leans against the counter, fighting her mind's desire to replay the events of the night before. The woman looks out the window at the leaves of the large chestnut oak in the backyard shining a brilliant green in the slanting sunlight. That is when she is struck by an idea. The woman tries to ignore it but she cannot get rid of it, the idea springing back into her thoughts again and again like gum stuck to her shoe. She pours two cups of coffee and decides to discuss her idea with her husband. By the time she reaches the bedroom, her hands are trembling so violently that coffee sloshes over the edges of each cup, spattering the hardwood floor.

After more than an hour of discussion—neither coffee touched—the man and woman hear their daughter's bedroom door open and the light padding of the girl's feet as she goes to the bathroom. The mother and father rise and begin to get dressed.

When they are ready, the man and woman knock on the girl's door. There's no answer, but the woman eases it open and peeks inside to make sure the girl is dressed. The girl is sitting on her bed, still in pajamas, staring at her cell phone. She glances at her parents for a moment before returning her attention to the phone's screen. Her mother perches on the edge of the bed, and her father stands at the bed's end, gripping the rail of the end board hard enough to blanch his fingers. The girl's parents explain—the mother doing most of the talking—that since it's the first day in a long time that the sun is out and the weather is pleasant, they think it would be nice to take a drive up to the mountains and perhaps have a picnic. The girl, to the surprise of her parents, immediately says yes—anything to get out of this house. The mother and father smile and leave the girl alone to get dressed. When they step into the hallway and close the girl's door, they look at each other, smiles melted, and hug.

It's a two-hour drive to the place the man's boss had told him about when they had discussed their mutual love of trout fishing. Most people in these mountains like to fish the French Broad, but this spot is on the Pigeon River, which is smaller and less well-known. The boss had said it was very isolated, that he'd never seen any other people there in the dozens of times he'd fished there, and that if you want peace and privacy, this is the spot.

During the drive, there is almost no conversation. The girl sits in the backseat, listening through earbuds to music on her iPhone. Her parents sit up front, silent, as if they're afraid speaking will shatter the momentum of the day. The man double-checks the directions he printed off the computer before leaving Winston-Salem. He asks his wife to keep an eye out for a truck repair shop that is about thirty yards from the turnoff they need to take. Fifteen minutes later, they find the location they're searching for. It is exactly as the man's boss described. A small, shaded clearing splits the trees that line the river, which is swollen and turbulent after a week of incessant rain. The rush of the water is loud and oddly different from the sound of the ocean they are used to hearing from spending so many years on the coast. It sounds angrier, the woman thinks, and more urgent.

The man and woman unpack the car. They spread a blanket about fifteen feet from the edge of the riverbank and lay out the containers of fried chicken, potato salad, and coleslaw they picked up at Harris Teeter on the way out of town. They all kick off their shoes and sit. The woman fixes a plate for the girl, who is staring at the river, mesmerized. The water is scary-looking, the girl tells her parents. Her father explains that it's not always like this. Most of the time, he has been told, it's peaceful and slow. The girl nibbles on a chicken thigh and eats potato salad with a plastic spoon while her parents pick at their food. The man and woman are watching the river. Soon, the man taps his wife on the arm, and she nods without turning to him. The girl's parents walk down to the edge of the water. It's a hot day with an expected high of ninety degrees but the soft, glistening mud of the bank is cool, squishing between their toes. The pounding water sounds like a train rushing past them.

The man calls back to the daughter, urging her to come wet her feet. It's so hot, he says, and the water is nice and cool. The girl laughs and says she's too afraid. But the man and woman both cajole the girl until she relents and joins them down by the river's edge. The mother takes hold of the girl's right hand and the father grabs her left, each parent assuring the girl that she is safe.

Overhead, a hawk rides a thermal in a sweeping arc. The girl notices it and can see the orange-red of its tail against the bright sky. She follows the bird's flight as it soars above and behind where they are standing.

The girl is still trying to follow the path of the hawk when she hears her father begin to count. She turns back to ask why he is counting, but suddenly pressure on her back propels her forward, and her head is under the cold water. She struggles to get up, but for some reason, she can't. Something heavy stops her. Panic takes hold, and the girl squirms to free herself. She twists enough to see her father next to her, and his hand comes down to press against the side of her face, keeping her under the water. The girl tries to kick her legs, but other hands (Mommy?) are gripping them tight. Then, all at once, she needs to take a breath, the urgency building in her, replacing all of her questions about why this is happening. Everything becomes unimportant except the desire to breathe, to get some small gulp of air, to keep her nose and mouth closed even though she is desperate to open them just a little. The water is strong, slamming against her, wanting to get inside her before the air can, and the girl knows she can't let that happen no matter what. But then she feels her nose open, and the water tickles at first and then burns, and it makes her want to cough, and she does, and water floods into her mouth, and soon the water all around her gets slowly darker and darker, and then becomes black and finally, a brilliant white, and it is then that the girl feels the water's comforting warmth and realizes that the river loves her more than she's ever been loved before.

When the girl stops moving, her mother and father stand up. The woman is sobbing, and the man cannot stop shaking. The woman stumbles out of the water and falls to her knees in the soft mud while the girl's father lifts their daughter's body to the surface. He kisses his daughter on the forehead and wades out into the river. He staggers as the rough undercurrent smacks his legs, knocking into him. He stumbles and his head slips briefly under the surface. When he rights himself, he is up to his thighs. He pushes the girl toward the center of the river. Her limp body is grabbed by the rapids and pulled instantly downriver. The man watches his daughter's body dip and rise as it is carried away.

Back on shore, the man pulls his wife up by her shoulders and tells her she has to make the call, that she has to make it now, or the plan will fall apart. He retrieves the girl's cell phone from the picnic blanket, dials 911, and places the phone in his wife's hand before walking back to the water's edge to wait for help.

The man stands in the middle of their new living room, surrounded by dozens of unpacked moving boxes. He is exhausted—not by the easy drive from Wilmington, but by the fact that this is their third move in less than two years. Maybe, he tells himself, relocating inland (away from the sweltering beach and closer to the cool mountains) will be the change they all need. Unconvinced, he begins ripping the strapping tape off a box marked "LAMPS, LIVING ROOM."

Two hours later, when his wife and daughter return from shopping, the man has arranged all the furniture and unloaded the boxes from the living and dining rooms. Experience has made him efficient, he tells his wife, and they laugh, but it is hollow. Their daughter stomps upstairs to her bedroom so she can watch YouTube videos on her laptop. The man and woman work, emptying boxes in the kitchen. As she places the utensil tray in one of the drawers beneath the counter and fills it, the woman sighs when she sees the empty knife slots next to the neatly arranged spoons and forks.

It's been so long now that the girl's parents can scarcely remember when the real troubles started. Their daughter was a fussy baby, but that's not uncommon. The first noticeable signs of serious problems occurred in preschool. The girl would squabble with the other children, push them, and hit them, and break their things. One day, she tried to bite her teacher. And while the staff was patient, her frequent disruptions eventually made it necessary to take her out of the school. The girl's parents were diligent, reading book after book, but the solutions offered were unsuccessful in curbing the girl's antisocial behavior. Then came a series of child psychologists who also had little effect. The family would move to another nearby town to try a new school. When that proved unsuccessful, or they were asked to leave, they'd move again. Then, inexplicably, for a short period, while the girl was in the second and third grades, there was a real hope that her behavior was finally getting better.

But that ended when her mother found the birds. Straightening the girl's bedroom one morning while her daughter was at school, the woman detected an odd odor coming from near the bed. Looking underneath it, she noticed a shoebox. When she lifted the lid, the woman shrieked and dropped the box, spilling a dozen dead birds—mostly cardinals and robins, but there was a goldfinch and a chickadee, as well—all headless. The woman confronted the girl after school, and the girl calmly explained that the birds were saying bad things about her, calling her filthy names, and telling her to do mean things. She explained that cutting their heads off was the only way to shut them up. The girl was punished, but her mother would soon find more birds and, eventually, chipmunks and voles and small rabbits. This was the moment the man and woman became truly frightened.

They tried medication, but other than making the girl sleep more, none of it helped. The turning point came one day in the fifth grade as the girl sat bored by her teacher's explanation of fractions. She reached into her book bag and retrieved the knife she'd taken from the kitchen that morning. While the teacher explained that one-fourth and three-twelfths were equivalent fractions, the girl reached around the side of the desk and stabbed the thigh of the boy sitting in front of her. It was later discovered that the knife had only just missed piercing an artery, which might have been fatal. The police became involved, and when questioned as to why she did it, the girl said only that she didn't like the boy's shirt and was sick of having to look at it all day.

The girl's animosity focused on her parents after she was forced to stay home (she'd been kicked out of school again and would have to repeat the fifth grade somewhere else the following year). The girl began to talk about all the people who needed to die—neighbors, the mailman, the president—and when the next-door neighbor's affable old Labrador retriever was found strangled with the girl's jump rope, the man and woman knew it was time for them to do something drastic. Her parents struggled, however, to know what was best for everyone. They conferred with a number of psychiatrists, the majority of whom recommended institutionalization and monitoring. One doctor, though, mentioned a new program operated through Baptist Hospital in Winston-Salem that worked with disturbed children. The program had had some success with children like their daughter. The girl's parents arranged to get her an evaluation and began looking for a house there.

Looking up from the utensil drawer, the woman peers out the window facing the backyard. A massive oak tree shades this side of the house. It's beautiful and peaceful, she thinks. The previous owners had built a large fishpond but had taken their fish when they'd left. The woman can just make out the edge of the pond in the corner of the yard beyond the tree. *I wonder if fish would be safe to have.*

Two months later, on a rainy Saturday night, the girl and her parents are sitting in the basement family room watching a movie—a comedy—and waiting for the pizza they've ordered. It's been tranquil since the move to Winston-Salem and the parents' hopes are high that this has been the final, effective move that will straighten out their lives. The man and woman sit on each end of the sofa. The girl is on the floor, positioned between her parents, with her back against the sofa. On the TV, an actor drives a car into a swimming pool, and the man and woman laugh while the girl says in an even tone that she is going to kill them both. The father mutes the television. He asks the girl to repeat what she just said. In the same flat tone, she informs her parents that one night, while they're asleep, she will come into their bedroom and kill them. This is too much for the man, who reaches down, grabs the girl's shoulder, and slaps her hard across the cheek. Dark red streaks appear on her pale skin. He yells at her that she is evil, that she has ruined their lives, even though he and her mother have given her nothing but love and support. He tells the girl that she needs to grow up and stop acting out. The woman jumps up and pulls her husband's hand from where he is still gripping the girl. She pleads with him to calm down, but just then, the girl begins keening and starts punching her mother's back. Instinctively, the woman shoves her daughter away, and when she does, the girl falls hard onto her back, her head smacking against the hard tile floor.

The girl gets up holding the back of her head and snatches the TV remote off the sofa. She hurls it through the small window directly behind the couch. Rain splatters the windowsill. The girl then walks over and pulls down the large television, the screen shattering with a muffled explosion. Her father rushes over and takes hold of the girl's arm to control her. The girl begins slapping at him, but he pulls her over and shoves her onto the couch, which is sprinkled with small shards of glass. Her father fights to control his rage. Her mother holds her hands over her face, sobbing.

The girl looks up at her parents and, in the same tone of voice in which she announced she planned to murder them, says she is sorry and that she doesn't know why she does these things. "Can't you help me?" she pleads.

The woman sits down next to her daughter and pulls her close. A few minutes later, the woman leads the girl upstairs to bed. The man stays to fit a board into the broken window until it can be replaced.

By the time the man gets upstairs to the bedroom, his wife is sitting on the edge of their bed. She's taken off her jeans and top and is wearing only her bra and panties. After he closes the bedroom door, she tells him to put a chair under the knob to block it; otherwise, she will not be able to sleep. He starts to protest but slides a high-back chair from the corner and angles it under the knob. The man and woman sit together on the bed and discuss their daughter. They've lost her, they agree. The girl will have to be sent away. They are out of options. What else can they do? She's a danger to them and to everyone—even to herself.

The man shuts off the lamp beside the bed, but his wife begs him to leave it on. They lie in bed, each lost in their own thoughts, listening to the light patter of the rain against the windows. After twenty minutes, the man is snoring, but the woman continues to lie awake, unable to sleep.

She remembers the day her daughter was born. . .

The obstetrician hands her their daughter mere moments after she has given birth. The baby's whole body is wet and messy, and she is crying. The woman holds her new daughter against her breasts, smiling at her husband, who is standing next to the bed with tears in his eyes. The baby continues to wail. For a moment her face turns bright red as she tries to catch her breath. The mother presses her daughter's head against her, and the baby quiets.

Return to Harmony

The small town where I'd grown up hadn't been on my mind for a long time when I received the phone call from Ken Browder saying someone was interested in buying my father's mobile home and the quarter-acre lot on which it sat rotting. The money being offered wasn't much, but then it wasn't worth much. Truth be told, getting rid of the property would be the final step in erasing Harmony from my life, and I considered that payment enough.

I turn onto Avery Lane, a dusty dirt road marked with a tilted road sign. A minute later I reach the U-shaped driveway of my father's neglected trailer, my wheels crunching loudly on the chert rock as I pull up front. I step carefully on the rickety aluminum steps and lift the flap on the mailbox to retrieve the key. After I unlock the door I step back to let out the hot, fetid air before I step into the single-wide. On the floor in the middle of the filthy trailer are two cardboard boxes into which Ken Browder has gathered all that remains of my father's forgotten possessions. One box is sealed with wide strips of packing tape, the word CLOTHES written across the top in black marker. The other box is open, and jutting out of the top is the trophy I'd won when my Little League Juniors Division team won the county championship the summer I turned thirteen. When I lift the side flap of the box I glance at a jumble of my father's personal effects, the sole remains of the man's life in Harmony. I halfheartedly rummage through them, stopping a moment to lift out a framed photograph of my mother, who'd died of a heart attack when I was six. I have a copy of the same picture back in my apartment in Winston-Salem. As always I'm struck by the resemblance to my own daughter, Penny, who lives with her mother in Raleigh.

I carry the boxes out to the car and put them in the trunk before taking a final walkthrough of my father's empty mobile home. Other than a sprinkling of rat shit, I find only a half-empty tin of Skoal under the bathroom sink. I leave it there and walk out and relock the door, replacing the key in the mailbox.

On my way back to the interstate, I approach the Kozy Kafé, whose brick exterior, painted fire engine red, is the only dash of color in the row of drab buildings at the town's center. I'm seized by an urge to pull in and get something to eat, certain it's the last time I'll be in Harmony. I angle into the gravel parking lot on the side of the building. There's only one other car there. When I walk in I half expect to see Lucy Wallace to be standing in the middle of the restaurant in her sky-blue polyester pantsuit holding a big plastic pitcher of sweet tea. Instead, the only people there are an old couple I don't recognize sitting at one of the booths lining the wall to my right, and a plump teenage girl behind the long counter to my left. The air is heavy with the odor of stale grease, and I find it oddly comforting.

"Sit anywhere," the girl says.

The elderly couple watches me as I walk to the counter and take the stool closest to the door. The waitress comes over and slides a menu in front of me.

"What can I get you to drink?" she asks.

"Sweet tea, please."

I glance at the menu only long enough to confirm the Kozy Burger—a burger piled high with chili and slaw—is still listed. When she comes back with my tea I order the burger medium-well, with fries.

The girl starts to walk away. "Excuse me, Miss," I say. "Does Lucy Wallace still work here?"

She looks at me then and there's a hesitation as she studies my face, trying to place me. "Mrs. Wallace passed two years ago. Her son, Carter, took over. He's in the back cooking. You want to talk to him?"

"No, thanks," I say, a little too quickly. "I used to live in Harmony. When I was young, Mrs. Wallace was a fixture here. I was just curious, is all."

The girl nods and walks away, disappearing through a swinging door past the far end of the counter. A minute later Carter Wallace steps through the same door. I recognize him easily enough but he's gone soft, with a large potbelly and pendulous jowls and little trace of the star quarterback I remember except for prominent biceps pinched in the sleeves of his T-shirt. Stretched across his front is a liberally stained white apron. All the time he's approaching I can tell he's trying to recognize me.

"Hey there," Carter says. "Brandi says you were asking after my mother. Do I know you?"

I realize I've been holding my breath and I let it out slowly. "Well, we were in high school together, you and me."

"You do look kinda familiar. What's your name?"

"Tanner Vance."

I was nobody to Carter Wallace back in high school, one of a hundred nameless faces he barely acknowledged because I wasn't a jock or one of the cool kids.

"Oh, yeah," he says. "You always hung out with Gareth Boger."

My stomach tightens at the mention of Gareth's name and neither of us says anything for a minute.

One night, after we'd had an argument, I left Gareth to run alone toward town while I went straight home. My father still owned the small farm off Powell Road I'd grown up on, so when I got there I went upstairs to my bedroom on the back side of the house. The next morning was the beginning of harvest, so I knew my old man would be sound asleep. My bedroom's window looked out on the fifty or so acres we split between tobacco and soybeans. When I was little, every year around this time in early July when both crops were ready for harvesting, I would sit on the end of my bed and gaze out at the vast, emerald fields and be grateful for the view. But that night I was drunk and tired, and after stripping down to my underwear I flopped onto my bed, falling fast asleep within minutes. I never heard the wail of the many sirens that night.

Next morning, on Saturday, I went downstairs to the kitchen expecting to find my father filling thermoses with coffee, which he'd always had ready by the time I got up. He wasn't there. My head was killing me so I went to pour a cup, but there was no coffee. Since we were harvesting soybeans that day, I concluded my father had just been anxious to get started and was out in the big shed readying the harvester. I stepped out on the back steps and listened. Mourning doves cooed from a nearby telephone line, but otherwise I heard nothing. I hollered in the direction of the shed, but my old man never appeared. It was at that moment I realized the air had an odd odor, like chimney smoke, but who on earth would be using a fireplace in July? When I went back into the kitchen I heard the rumble of my dad's truck pulling into the driveway. A few moments later the front door screen banged shut and he walked into the kitchen, the strong smell of smoke trailing him like a faithful dog.

"What's going on?" I asked.

"You were dead asleep, but at about two this morning I was woke up by a bunch of sirens. I pulled on some clothes and when I got in my truck I could see the glow of fire over towards town. By the time I got to where it was, Clyde Wallace's store was up in flames."

I felt like all the blood had plummeted to my feet and I became woozy. I began to tremble and had to grab the edge of the kitchen's small Formica-topped table for fear I'd fall over. I sat down.

"You okay, son?" my father asked.

I nodded weakly. "What happened?"

"No one knows yet. They only just now got the fire put out. Clyde's got loads of flammables there, and one of the firemen I was talkin' to thinks maybe, 'cause it's been so damned hot of late, something overheated and exploded. When things cool down they should be able to tell for certain what happened."

The stench of the smoke clinging to my father's clothes was overwhelming and I lurched to the sink and vomited. The mess reeked of beer and Kozy Kafé cheeseburger, and smelling it caused me to heave again.

"Looks like someone and his buddies partied a little too much last night," my father said.

I rinsed out the sink, cupped my hands and sipped some cool water. When I felt I was able, I stood and turned to see my father staring at me.

"Drinking too much ain't gettin' you out of your chores, mister," he said. "I'm going out to the shed and start the harvester. You meet me there when you get cleaned up. You might want to make some coffee first."

I nodded and he walked out the back door, thankfully taking the odor of the burned feed store with him. When I was back in my bedroom I considered calling Gareth, but at that moment I realized things had changed forever.

For weeks, the fire was all anyone in Harmony talked about. The fire chief from Statesville came to take charge of investigating the cause of the blaze. He'd determined the fire had started in the back of the building, where hay bales were stored. No flammable substances or accelerants were detected, yet there was no reason the hay should have spontaneously combusted so that's when the possibility of arson was considered and the FBI brought in. In the end, nothing conclusive was ever found. Clyde Wallace told the police he couldn't think of anyone who held a grudge against him. Eventually, life went back to normal for most of Harmony's four hundred residents. That is, until eight months later when Carter Wallace's father blew his own head off.

"What brings you back to Harmony?" Carter asks, wiping his hands with the hem of his cook's apron.

"Just collecting some things from my old man's place that just got sold."

Carter nods and there's a pause as we each struggle for small talk.

"Well, I best get back there and check your burger. Wouldn't want it to overcook. Nice seein' you, Tanner."

"Thanks, Carter. Same here."

He retreats to the kitchen and Brandi comes over with my glass of iced tea.

"On second thought, let me get my food to go, please," I say.

Brandi brings the food and the bill. Even though the total is only $8.50 I hand her a twenty and tell her to keep the change. I walk out into the bright sunlight both relieved and a little sad knowing this will be the last time I ever come to the Kafé.

I pull back onto Harmony Highway and turn south toward the Interstate. Soon I see ahead on my right the abandoned lot where the Wallaces' feed store sat. Clyde Wallace's insurance wasn't nearly enough to cover the loss and he never rebuilt the store. When I reach the site, I am unable to keep from stopping. My tires kick up a cloud of red dust when I pull onto the empty dirt clearing. I sit in the car, sweating despite having set the dashboard air conditioning vents on high.

In the distance, beyond the road on the right, lurking like a silent watchman, is the town's water tower, whose giant steel legs made a convenient and secluded place where Gareth and I could hang out summer nights after work to drink beer or smoke a joint. The night the feed store burned down, Gareth and I were sitting on the grass beneath the tower, our backs against the warm steel, relaxing after a particularly hard day of re-tarring the roof of the municipal building. That summer we'd gotten part-time jobs doing maintenance for the town manager, Dennis Tomlinson. The sky was gray, the color of ashes, and fighting to hold onto the last of the day's light. By the time we popped open our fourth can of beer, it was full dark and mosquitoes and gnats buzzed around us, invisible in the humid air. Even though he couldn't have been more than a dozen feet away from me, Gareth was an indistinct shadow. As usual, Gareth did most of the talking. He prattled on and on about what a prick Mr. Tomlinson was and what a shithole place Harmony was and how he hated everything about it, and the drunker Gareth got, the number of things and people he despised grew exponentially. I, for the most part, kept silent, nodding occasionally in case he could still see me.

"Know who else is a douchebag?" he asked after a lull I had hoped meant his ranting was over for the night.

"Who?" I said.

"Carter Wallace. That dickhead thinks just because he's a starter on our piece of shit football team that he's so much better than us."

I never had a problem with Carter, who was Lucy and Clyde's son. I rarely spoke to him at school, and was going to say this to Gareth, but decided not to start an argument.

"Did I ever tell you what he said to me one day just before school ended this year?"

I shook my head and gulped my beer.

"Well," Gareth said, "I was walking down the hall headed to math class and accidentally bumped Carter's arm—his precious throwing arm I guess—so he shoves me against the lockers and says, 'You want to know why you and your friends are such shit, Boger? It's because y'all will never lose the stink of those dirty, worthless farms. You'll spend the rest of your miserable lives breathing in tractor fumes and dust from chicken shit all day. I read somewhere there's chemicals in that stuff that eats your brain away piece by piece. Then on Sunday afternoons, you'll be watchin' me and bragging to your rube buddies that you knew me back in the day.'" Gareth drained half a beer in one swallow. "Then he and his entourage start laughing like it was most clever thing they'd ever heard. Hell, it probably was."

"What did you do?" I asked.

"Nothing. Half the football team was with him. What could I do?"

I shrugged and swatted away a cloud of midges that had decided to check me out. Gareth was quiet a long while and I thought his anger at Carter Wallace had subsided, but then he stood up suddenly, and when he came to stand next to me he was swaying. He finished the beer he was working on, crushed the can, and threw it into the blackness beyond the water tower to land silently in the tall, unmown Johnson grass.

"Let's go," he said. "I've got an idea."

"Sit back down. Let's just finish our beers and enjoy the buzz."

"We can drink anytime. Right now we have to teach those Wallaces they aren't the kings of Iredell Fucking County."

"And how exactly do we do that?"

"Don't you worry. I got a plan."

We'd come in my truck, so whatever he was planning I'd have to drive. I envisioned Gareth wanting us to roll the trees in the Wallaces' yard or even something more vicious like hurl rocks through their windows. Maybe even slash tires on all their cars. But whatever he had in mind I had no desire to get involved.

"I'm going home," I said. "I'll drop you at your house."

"You're a real pussy, you know that?"

"Yeah, and I'm proud of it," I said, hoping to lighten the mood.

"Well, screw you, I can walk."

"Jesus, Gareth. Forget Carter Wallace. He's not worth our time. Let's just call it a night. I got to get up early tomorrow to help my dad cut beans." I could hear a hint of desperation in my voice and all at once I just wanted to be back home in my own bed.

Gareth flipped me the bird and started walking away. In moments I could no longer see him, but I heard the click and hiss as he opened his last beer. In my heart I knew I should follow him and continue to try and convince him to go home himself, but I was exhausted, so I walked to my truck. I had parked behind the tower, as inconspicuously as possible, and when I backed up to turn toward the road, my headlights landed briefly on Gareth, who had begun to run south down the side of Harmony Highway toward the center of town.

As I drive back through town, I notice in place of the town marker, sitting lopsided in a patch of weedy dirt, a portable illuminated business sign with a flashing arrow pointing north toward the town's heart, as if there was another direction anyone could go in Harmony. Eight-inch changeable letters announce multiple lots for sale, with information available at Browder Real Estate, 0.2 miles ahead.

Within a quarter of a mile the landscape shifts. Long, dense patches of shortleaf pines and white oaks hedge in the roadside, shielding farmhouses from the grime and noise of truck and tractor traffic. Short, unpaved lanes jut off from the main road, bearing the names of families who settled this area a hundred years ago or more—Ansley-Harding Way, York Lane, Boger Farm Road. Names that also belonged to our neighbors and the kids I used to know and who were my childhood friends. When I reach the rusty, dented sign directing people to the First Baptist Church on the right side of the road, I am unable to keep from looking in my rearview mirror one last time at the abandoned space where the feed store used to sit.

For several days immediately following the fire, Gareth had called me frequently. My father would leave notes on the kitchen table saying he'd phoned but I refused to return his calls. Although I'd done nothing wrong, I had never been as scared in my life as I was that summer. I called Mr. Tomlinson to tell him I was sorry but I couldn't come back to the job because of my responsibilities on the farm. I had no desire to see Gareth, at least until I had to when school started back at the end of August. It was our senior year but we didn't have any classes together and I was grateful for that. I'd see him occasionally in the hallways, of course, but whenever he called to me I would just walk away.

Then one March, a week before our spring break, Clyde Wallace committed suicide in his basement. The school was abuzz with gossip about it. Despite the fact that Gareth was never, to my knowledge, suspected of any involvement in the feed store fire, I knew I should say something to someone about that night at the water tower. But, like Gareth had said to me before he'd set off, I was a pussy.

Subsequently, my paranoia was such I was afraid to be seen even talking to Gareth. One day not long after that he chased after me between classes and pinned me against the lockers, his hands pressing hard into my shoulders.

"What the fuck is going on?" he asked. "Why are you ignoring me?"

I looked quickly around to see if anyone could hear us. "You really have to ask?"

Gareth didn't say anything right away, which told me he already knew why I was avoiding him.

"I need to talk to you, man," he said.

"Let's get it straight, Gareth. I don't know a thing. About anything. And I want to keep it that way. But I don't want to hang out with you anymore, get it? Leave me alone and I'll leave you alone."

He pulled his hands off me and took a step back. I ignored a sharp pain in my lower back where the handle of one of the lockers had pressed in.

"But I want to explain things to you. You're my best friend. I always could tell you anything."

"That's over, Gareth." I pushed past him and was surprised to feel tears burning my eyes. I wasn't so much sad as I was scared, because Gareth had just come as close to confessing his crime as I would ever hear.

Following that next summer I went to Chapel Hill to pursue a business degree at the University of North Carolina. I came back during summers to help my dad on the farm. During the break between my sophomore and junior years, I'd heard from some folks in town that Gareth had moved to Statesville to sell cars at the Ford dealership but he'd gotten his boss' daughter pregnant and disappeared one night without saying a word. Rumors placed him in various towns in the Midwest or Texas, depending on who was doing the telling. I'd be lying not to say I was relieved he'd left North Carolina.

Right after I graduated college, the economy tanked and my father had to sell the farm and move into the trailer while he took odd jobs. I'd gotten a position with a marketing firm in Winston-Salem and begged him to move there but he was stubborn and refused. For my part, I reasoned I was near enough to help him but far enough away to not have to think about Harmony. But when my father was diagnosed three years ago with lung cancer, I did move him to an eldercare facility in Winston-Salem. Two years ago he lost the battle. After my dad was gone I didn't think much about his trailer and the small lot it was on since he'd bought it all outright with proceeds from the sale of the farm. Until, that is, Ken Browder contacted me and said someone was interested in buying the property.

I accelerate to merge into the eastbound traffic on I-40, sensing the muscles of my arms relax. When I glance in the rearview mirror I can see the sign on the opposite side of the highway pointing in backward lettering to the exit for Harmony. The sign shrinks rapidly as I head away from it at seventy miles per hour, but I keep staring at it, almost expecting to see Clyde Wallace or Dennis Tomlinson or Gareth himself to step from behind it and beckon me back. But, of course, they don't.

The car is saturated with the pleasant, suety smell of the Kozy Burger, cooked by Carter Wallace himself, and I shake my head. Carter was so certain his talent on the football field would take him as far from Harmony as a person could go, while I always figured I'd end up following in my father's footsteps and take over the farm on Powell Road. Yet neither of us imagined that both of those things would change in the course of one calamitous night.

I take one last, quick glance in the mirror, but it isn't long before the highway curves, and Harmony, with all her ghosts, disappears for good.

For You

Dear Mr. Springsteen,
I know you get lots of mail (especially from women) but I want you to know that this is not a "fan letter," per say (Is that right? I'm a terible speller.). Not that I'm not a huge fan (Oh, boy, am I!) but the purpose of this letter is to tell you about a situation, which I'm sure is nothing to worry about, but maybe you should be aware of.

Let me state right up front that Ronnie, my husband, is a decent hard working man who would never harm a fly. Granted, he was a whole bunch sweeter twenty-three years ago when I married him, but even though he no longer seems to think it's important to remember "little" things, like our anniversary or my birthday (FYI, June 27), it's not like he hits me a lot or anything. Anyway, the point is you should know that, while I think it's all just talk, Ronnie has been saying things that could be interpreted by some people as threats.

I should mention here that Ronnie (unlike me) is not a fan of your music. Last week I came home with two copies of your new CD. (Just so you know, I always buy two—one for the house, one for the truck, which is probably good for sales, right? The thing is I have been listening to it pretty much nonstop. Holy cow! It is soooo good!!) and I think Ronnie has gotten jealous I don't spend more time with him, especially at night (if you know what I mean. I think you do.). So last night, after way too many beers, he says to me, "Goddammit, I'm warning you...You stop listening to that asshole's music, or I'm gonna do something." Or something along those lines. I can't remember it exactly as I must confess that I'd had a couple drinks, too (but not too many, I'm not like that).

Anyway, this morning Ronnie and the truck were gone when I got up and when I called Jiffy Lube they said he never even showed up for work. No doubt he's parked somewhere with a bottle of Jack, feeling bad about how mean he was. But I guess my point is I figured you might want to pass this information on to your security people. You know, just in case.

On a more upbeat note, I want to mention that I happen to be a pretty good singer myself. I know I'm not in your league, or even Patty's (she's got the voice of an angel, but you know that), but my friends and family have always said that I should be a profesional singer I'm so good. So if you ever need a backup singer, like in an emergency, I want you to know I am available ANY time. And just so you don't think I'm saying that to impress you, I've included a tape of me singing I Wanna Marry You, which is one of my ABSOLUTE favorites of yours (it is so sweet and sad all at the same time—how on earth do you do that?).

Sincerly,

A Fan

P.S. Please note that I did not sign this letter "Your BIGGEST Fan." My God, how many of those letters must you get, right? I hope that shows you that I am not one of those fanatics you must have to deal with every single day.

P.S.S. Sorry I couldn't sign my real name, but considering how Ronnie is, I think you can see it's for the best.

Dear Bruce Springsteen,

I didn't really expect you to reply to my letter right away (I know you are very busy with the tour and all), but I thought I should keep you posted on what is happening with Ronnie cause I feel you and your security people need to know. Despite some of those things I said about him in my last letter you have nothing to worry about. Turns out the lying bastard wasn't mad at me. He'd just gone and shacked up with another woman! And she aint nothing but a two-bit whore from The Doll House (that's this sleazy strip club he's always going to) and trust me, she isn't the good-hearted, just-trying-to-get-by kind, like in your song <u>Reno</u>. You know, I <u>had</u> been wondering why he stopped asking me to go there with him. Well, I guess I know now, don't I?

The thing that really pisses me off, though, is the fact that the damn truck he's driving is half mine. I put up the money for it back when I was working. If that motherfucker thinks he can just steal my half of the truck, then he's got another think coming. But hell, none of this is your problem, right? I just know you have a sensitive soul and are the kind of man (unlike Ronnie!) that would listen to his woman's troubles with a simpathetic ear. It shows in your music, by the way.

Did you get a chance to listen to my tape? I hope so. What did you think? The sound quality wasn't so good, I know, but I don't have fancy recording equipment like <u>some</u> people! I'm sending another tape with this letter because I realize that you can't really get a good idea about my voice in just one song. This time I'm singing <u>Dancing in the Dark</u> (another favorite!) because it has a faster tempo and shows you that I can really "rock" it. I'm still available anytime—now more than ever, I suppose (fuck you, Ronnie!), so just let me know. If it's more convenient for you, I <u>will</u> be attending your show in

Charlotte next month (as if I'd miss it!), so we can meet in person. That would be so cool.

A Fan

P.S. Sorry about the bad language in this letter, but considering some of your lyrics, I know you probably don't mind. :-)

P.S.S. If you <u>do</u> call me out at the concert, just use the name "Maranda." It's not my real name, but it can be our special code name.

Dear Bruce,

First of all, WHAT A SHOW! You were, as always, fantastick! You didn't even know that was me in the second row. I was the one with long red hair (I dyed mine right after I heard <u>Red Headed Woman</u>, not to mention you clearly have a thing for redheads—right, Patty?) and was wearing black jeans and the black Born in the USA t-shirt. At one point (during <u>Tenth Avenue Freeze-Out</u>) you looked <u>RIGHT AT ME!</u> I tried to get close to the stage to tell you who I was, but your security guys are real good at their job and pushed me back. By the way, the bald one did hurt my shoulder a little bit, but don't worry, I'm not going to sue you. Hee hee.

I was, as you can imagine, quite disapointed that you forgot to call out my name, but I'm okay. And just so you know, Ronnie is back. Whoop dee doo (sp.?)!! After I wrote you I confronted him about the truck at The Doll House, and I guess he decided I was right, and did what he thought was the right thing (for once). But I'm no sap, that's for sure. He thinks I've forgiven him, but what he doesn't know is that I fake the majority of my orgasims now. And truth be told, when I don't, it's usually because I'm pretending it's <u>you</u> on top of me instead of Ronnie. I hope that doesn't embarass you. I bet it doesn't.

Anyway, Ronnie told me that he's all through with that tramp (the <u>real</u> kind, not "tramps like us"! heh heh), but yesterday a friend told me that he saw her with him again just last week. I told him to get the hell out, once and for all, and not to come back, but that got him all mad and he started screaming and said he'll decide who stays and who goes in this house and got all up in my face and started to get rough with me, but luckily he passed out. I need to just leave that drunkin bastard and move away once and for all (hey! New Jersey isn't that far from North Carolina! haha). If there was any justice in this world, then one night he'd hit a tight curve a little too fast and all my worries would be over, right? (Hey! Just like your song <u>Wreck on the Highway</u>, huh?) I guess that sounds pretty bad to you, doesn't it? I hope you know I'm only kidding.

A Fan

P.S. Just so you know, I had to pay a FORTUNE to get such a good seat. I don't have that kind of money lying around, so I pawned Ronnie's shotgun to get it. He hasn't found out yet. It's our little secret, OK?

Hi, Bruce,

You probably thought I'd forgotten about you, it's been so long since I wrote. Things here have been a little hectic. Since my last letter, Ronnie has passed away. It's eerie (sort of), considering what I wrote in my last letter, but Ronnie actually <u>did</u> die in a car crash. Seems there was a small leak in the brake line and all the fluid drained out, so when he was going down Bald Mountain Road on the way to work (which you don't know, but it's VERY steep), he just couldn't stop. The officer who told me said he thought the truck hit the tree at over ninety miles per hour, but at least it was a blessing that Ronnie probably died instantanously. So, as you might suspect, I have had my hands full with funneral arrangements and paper work (you have NO idea the forms you have to fill out!!).

Enough about me. I bet you're pretty tired right about now. Are you glad the tour is over? Five months on the

road would kill most men (but then, you're not most men!).
Anyway, I hope you are getting some rest. Are you back in
New Jersey? I only ask because—guess <u>what</u>?!—I'm
moving to New York City. I've decided my family is right
and I should try to become a real singer. (Do you have the
names of any agents that are looking for new talent?) I
have included (yet) another tape with this letter in case
you wanted to pass it on to someone you know in the
business who might could help me. This time, I tried putting
a little country twist on your song <u>Waitin' on a Sunny Day</u>,
since I know that kind of "crossover" music is really
popular right now. I hope you don't mind. I know you
won't because you're such an angel (but not the kind that
Ronnie is right now, though—ooh. . .I'm bad!).

Well, I've got to go pack. I'm hoping to leave as soon as
the insurance check arrives (they said it should be sent early
next week), so if all goes well, I will be heading up north by
next Thursday. Are you going to be home? Ha, ha. . .just
kidding. Although, I really will be passing through New
Jersey <u>very</u> close to where you live (I bet celebrities like you
absolutely <u>hate</u> the Internet), so I was thinking I could stop
by. If you want to arrange a time, it would probably be best
for you to call me, rather than writing, since time will be too
short for a letter. You can reach me at 336-555-2882. If for
some reason I don't answer, just leave a message. And if you
hear a man's voice on the recording, don't worry. It's Ronnie's.
I'm using his cell phone (he won't need it anymore, right? heh
heh!). I just haven't figured out how to change the message.

Hope to see you soon.

Love,

Maranda

P.S. Tee hee. . .Maranda really IS my name. Did I fool
you?? I hope so.

P.S.S. What time does Patty take the kids to school? :-)

The Old Woman on the Porch

Late one morning on a cloudy October day, an old woman sits on the front porch of a weathered house that is nearly halfway along my route. A scruffy calico cat lies curled on her lap and the woman appears to be napping. Her head droops against her frail chest in such a way that I am able to see a pink circle of skin on the crown of her scalp. I take care to be as quiet as possible when I mount the steps to the porch but, despite my caution, my weight causes one of the boards to creak and the old woman lifts her head at the sound. The cat does not move.

"I have your mail, ma'am," I say.

I've been delivering this route for only a couple weeks and have never seen the old woman before.

"Thank you," she says in a raspy voice, barely louder than a whisper.

When she turns her face up to me I can see a grayish film covering both of her eyes and her gaze doesn't quite meet mine.

"I'm expecting a letter from my son," the old woman says. "He lives in California now. Los Angeles. He's got a very important job with a movie studio."

This is an obvious point of pride for her and she smiles. "Would you mind looking to see if it has come?" she asks.

I shuffle through the few envelopes, all bills. One is from the electric company with "FINAL NOTICE" stamped in red on the outside of the envelope.

"I'm sorry, ma'am, no letters today."

The old woman scratches the cat's head. I look at the animal, which remains curled in a ball. Its fur is ragged, sticking up in stiff clumps, and I can see the outline of ribs along its chest. I notice the old woman's tattered housedress as well, several dime-sized holes revealing chalky, bare skin beneath.

"Would you like me to slide your mail through the slot?" I ask.

"Thank you, dear. That would be fine. I'd hate to disturb Miss Puss here."

Just then a stiff breeze crosses the porch, cool enough to raise gooseflesh on my arms.

"It's a bit chilly to be sitting outside, don't you think?" I ask. "Perhaps you'd be more comfortable in the house."

"I'll go in soon, young man. But first I am waiting for the mailman to come by. I'm expecting a letter from my son. He lives in Los Angeles. He has a big job in the movies."

"*I'm* the mailman, ma'am. And your son's letter didn't come today. But maybe it will come tomorrow."

She looks at me blankly with those milky eyes and I can't discern whether she comprehends what I'm saying.

"I can help you inside, if you'd like," I say.

"Miss Puss here doesn't like to be disturbed."

"I'm sure Miss Puss would like to go inside, too," I say. "Cats crave warmth, after all."

A car backfires at the end of the block and I look down the street, anxious to finish my route. But it's getting colder and I hate to leave the old woman sitting alone in her confused state.

"Would Miss Puss let me pick her up?" I ask. "I can carry her inside for you."

"She's timid of strangers," the old woman says. "I wouldn't want her to scratch you."

"I'll be careful."

"Well, it *is* getting cool and Miss Puss does hate the cold weather."

I set my mailbag down next to the front door and walk over to where the woman sits. The cat never stirs at my approach.

"Easy, Miss Puss," I say. "I'm just going to take you inside."

I slide one hand under the cat's chest, the other under its hindquarters, and lift her off the old woman's lap. As I do I became aware of a revolting limpness in the cat's entire body and the animal's head flops over my wrist. Drops of clear fluid spill from its nostrils onto the cracked and peeling porch boards. I nearly drop the dead cat in my surprise.

"She likes to sleep along the back of the sofa," the old woman says. "So if you don't mind, put her up there. Plus, the others don't bother her so much when she's up high like that."

The old woman reaches up a spindly arm, moving it back and forth blindly until it locates the cat dangling in my hands and runs her fingers along the bumps of the animal's protruding backbones.

"Ma'am, I'm afraid Miss Puss has passed away," I say. I'm suddenly aware of my heart beating.

"Nonsense. She's just a sound sleeper, that's all."

"She isn't breathing. I'm very sorry."

The old woman doesn't respond and I watch her smooth her housedress with thin fingers whose knuckles look painfully knobby.

"Is there a blanket or something I can wrap her in?" I ask.

"Just leave her here," she says, and pats her lap. "I'll take her inside before long. As soon as the mailman comes by. He's going to bring me a letter from my son."

I walk down the porch steps and lay the dead cat behind an azalea bush in front of the railing. I stand for a moment, considering what I should do. After retrieving my mailbag I step over to the old woman once again.

"Good morning, ma'am," I say. "It's the mailman. I put your mail in the house for you."

"Oh, good morning," she says. "Is there by any chance a letter from California?"

"Actually, I think there is. Let's see. Yes, it's from Los Angeles."

"That's from my son," she says with more vigor than I'd heard in her voice yet and she begins to push herself out of the chair. She teeters a moment then sits back down.

"He's got a big job in the movies," she says softly, but no longer to me.

After several minutes, her head begins to droop again, and very soon her breathing takes on the distinct rhythm of sleep. I watch her for several minutes, pondering my responsibility and options. At last, I go to the door and lift the mail slot to drop in the old woman's mail. Hot, rancid air escapes through the opening, heavy with the smell of ammonia. And something else, something thick and nauseating.

As I make my way down the porch steps I dial the police on my cell phone. I convince myself there is nothing more I can do. I take a few steps across the dry patch of lawn separating the old woman's property from her neighbor's driveway, aware of the weight of my mailbag against my shoulder, but I stop when an officer answers my call and I explain the situation. A patrol car is being dispatched. Although I am anxious to finish my route, I go back and sit on the top step of the old woman's porch to wait. After a few minutes, the old woman shifts and begins to mutter, her eyes still closed. I have to lean toward her to make out her words.

"Be patient, Miss Puss. We'll go inside when the mailman arrives with our letter."

There is nothing more I can do for her, I tell myself as I sit in the cool breeze, desperately trying to ignore the continuous, high-pitched meowing coming from inside the house.

What Courage Looks Like

I had known Richie Logan since high school and as I sat at the bar at Finnigan's Wake, finishing off my second beer, I was beginning to think he wasn't going to show. It had been a good nine or ten years since I'd seen Richie but we'd exchanged emails occasionally and razzed each other often enough on Facebook, although not in some time. Yet I was somewhat surprised when he called me to say he was headed down to Boca Raton from his home in Massachusetts, planned on passing through Winston-Salem and hoped we could get together for a couple hours. I was about to signal the bartender to close out my tab when Richie tapped me on the shoulder, causing me to jump.

When I swiveled to face him I could tell easily enough it was him, but I was still stunned by how much he'd changed. He'd always been husky, if not fat, and I was struck by how much weight he'd lost since I last saw him. And the Richie that was fixed in my memory was always smiling. Everything, it seemed, would amuse him, no matter how stupid or dull the rest of us thought it was. But looking up at his face from my stool that hot July evening, I saw no smile, despite his obvious effort at one.

"Hey, Jacko," he said, using a nickname for me from our freshman year in high school.

I stood and we hugged before he plopped onto the stool next to mine. It was a Wednesday and the bar was sparsely populated with regulars. I ordered another Guinness and asked Richie if he wanted one too. We shared many pints back in college. He shook his head and asked the bartender to bring him a double martini, no garnish. I couldn't remember Richie ever drinking anything other than beer. Over the next hour we drank and talked about jobs and kids (we both had two in college now) and reminisced about all the stuff we had done so long ago, the memories of good times we carried into middle age. I was careful to avoid asking about Leanne, having heard from a mutual friend their marriage had been going through a rough patch in the past year, even if I didn't know any details. But after Richie's second martini he seemed to relax a bit and I decided it would be okay to ask how Leanne was doing. Richie looked up at me with what seemed a mixture of expectation and relief. Then he nodded and excused himself and headed for the men's room. While he was gone I ordered us another round. When Richie returned he pulled out his cell phone and navigated to a photograph of Leanne standing in their backyard, facing away from the camera.

"This is the last photograph I took of her, Jack," he said.

I looked at the picture a long time, considered the emphasis he'd put on the word "last," and assumed that things in their marriage had gone bad enough for them to separate. I handed the phone back to Richie and waited for him to tell his story. But he sat there silently for a long time staring at Leanne's picture. Off in the corner of the pub, by the dartboards, a girl squealed as she hit the bull's-eye. As I waited for Richie to speak I tried to remember the last time I'd seen Richie's wife. I figured it was six years ago, at our twentieth college reunion.

The night that Richie met Leanne we were all at a party at the off-campus house of some guys Richie knew. We were both juniors at Duke. The party was nothing special, the usual crowd of students walking around with cups of beer or huddled in small groups shouting over Duran Duran blasting from stereo speakers in the corner. I was on my fourth or fifth beer just shooting the shit with Richie and some other friends when I noticed Richie's attention lock on something behind me. I turned to see a girl filling her cup at the keg parked by the front door. Her back was to us, but her blonde hair was tied in a long ponytail that poked from the back of what turned out to be an Atlanta Braves ballcap. She had on tight jeans and a white T-shirt that she'd cut off at the midriff. When she turned, I thought she was pretty enough, but for the next twenty minutes Richie couldn't take his eyes off her, watching her circulate the party. Finally, I urged him to go speak to her, something Richie normally had no trouble doing. But there was something different about Leanne for him and eventually I had to physically push him at her before he'd approach her. I won't say it was love at first sight for Leanne, like it was for Richie, but they hit it off and dated steadily over the next two years. After graduation, Richie proposed and he'd agreed to move to Boston, near her parents. The three of us would visit each other a few times a year at first, but then I met Barbara, we all started having families, and our get-togethers dwindled to occasionally and then to rarely. But in all the ensuing years since college, I'd always thought Richie and Leanne had a solid marriage.

Richie seemed reluctant to stop looking at Leanne's photograph on his phone.

"You don't have to talk about it if you'd rather not," I said.

Richie looked up then and I could tell he was struggling not to cry. I regretted ordering another round of drinks.

"The thing is, Jack," he said at last, "Leanne is dead."

"Oh, shit, Richie. I am so sorry." I felt a trembling coldness in my chest.

He looked around and pointed to an empty table near the front door. We carried our drinks over and again I waited for Richie to speak first.

The trouble began about eighteen months before, he said, when his real estate agency hired a new broker named April. She was real green, just out of college, and had only acquired her realtor's license the week prior to starting with them. At the time April started, there were no problems with his marriage to Leanne. The housing market had yet to drop off the cliff, he was selling well and they were just learning to enjoy their recently empty nest. But Richie found himself instantly attracted to April, much in the way he had with Leanne. April wasn't the polar opposite of Leanne, but to Richie's mind she possessed those nebulous qualities he desired in a woman and that he'd secretly thought his wife lacked. April wore her dark brown hair either up in a bun or down loose around her shoulders. She was always dressed in business suits that looked expensive to Richie, but more importantly, showed off her long legs and great ass. Richie found himself hanging around the office, making himself available to help April get the swing of things. After a few weeks they'd met regularly for lunch and by the time she'd worked at his firm for six months, and despite an eighteen-year age difference, Richie told me, they'd fallen in love.

According to Richie, being a realtor made arranging trysts with April easy. On those nights he planned on seeing her, he'd simply tell Leanne it was the only time a client could meet him to view a house. Plus, there were always empty properties to which he had access. In the beginning,

Richie said, he and April would have sex as many as five or six days a week, often on the floor of empty houses. There was never a thought that he no longer loved Leanne, Richie added. He'd just found someone else who seemed to appreciate him in a different way, a way that made him feel young again. He was the happiest he had been in a very long time. And it seemed if he continued to be careful, he could have the best of both worlds.

Richie shook his head. "Like so many other guys, I believed what I wanted to believe," he said. "I am an idiot."

I nodded and told him I understood exactly how he felt, even though I didn't. He looked at me and I could tell he knew I was lying.

"Well, I guess I should tell you the bad part now," he said.

Despite all of April's assurances that she would never tell anyone about their affair, she did precisely that. One night April and some of the other women in the office went for a girls' night out. After several Cosmopolitans, April confided she had slept with Richie. It was not long after this that Leanne received an anonymous phone call telling her that her husband was sleeping with a young agent in his firm. Richie believes he knows who made the call, a partner whom he had clashed with on several occasions, but it didn't matter in the long run. Leanne confronted him. Richie denied it and claimed the phone call was from a rival agent who claimed he'd sold a house out from under her, but it wasn't long before Richie was forced to confess the truth. For his part, he said, he sincerely intended to end the affair. He loved Leanne as much as ever and wanted to save the marriage. He would quit the real estate firm, he told her, and find another company to work for. He even offered to see a marriage counselor.

But Leanne was devastated by the betrayal. She stopped leaving the house and for two weeks she didn't shower or bathe. Richie could not convince her to eat. Occasionally she would venture out to the backyard and just stand in one place for an hour or more. It was one of those times Richie had taken her picture, he said. Then one Monday at noon, he came home after interviewing for a position with another firm in town but he couldn't find Leanne. He searched every room in the house, repeatedly dialing her cell phone and getting no answer. Her car was in the driveway, so he wondered if maybe she'd decided to go next door to their friends' house. Just as Richie was walking toward the front door, he passed the door to the basement and realized he'd not looked down there. He was on the bottom step when he saw Leanne hanging from a water pipe, her face purple and bulging, the green wire of an extension cord cutting into the flesh of her neck. He told me he knew she was already dead, but he explained how he rushed over to her, tripping on the kitchen chair that was flipped over on the floor, and struggled to lift her weight so he could unknot the cord. He had to leave her body swinging from the pipe to run back upstairs and get a knife from the kitchen in order to cut her down. He called 911 and sat on the floor with Leanne's head on his lap until the paramedics came and pronounced her dead.

"There was no note," Richie said.

I was too shocked to even nod.

We finished our drinks and Richie told me he had to get back on the road. He thanked me for coming out and listening to his horror story. It helped to talk about it, he said. He was heading to Florida to stay with his brother and sister-in-law since he found it too uncomfortable living in Massachusetts. I tried to convince him to spend the night with Barbara and me, that he'd had too much to drink and he could leave early the next morning. But he insisted he wanted to get down the road a ways before stopping for the night. Part of me understood this.

I settled the bar tab and walked Richie to his car, which was parked around the block. The air was still muggy as we shuffled along the sidewalk, and I felt a heaviness settle on me that I knew had nothing to do with the weather. We hugged and Richie got into his car and powered down the window.

"I killed her," he said. "I know it and I just wanted someone else to know it. You've always been one of my best friends, Jacko. Thanks again for meeting me and for listening."

"I'll be right here anytime you need me. But do me a favor, will you? Call me when you get to Florida, okay?"

Richie said he would, then pulled the car out of the spot and drove down 7th Street. I watched until he turned at the corner, onto Cherry Street, headed for the interstate. As I made my way back toward Finnigan's where my own car was parked, I thought how Richie must lie in bed every night, unable to sleep, his mind focused on a series of horrible images—Leanne, her distorted and grotesque face hanging from the pipe, the weight of her head on his lap as he waited for help to arrive, that final photograph of her in the backyard forever turned away from him. I also thought about how his face looked just before he drove away, his expression telling me that he'll never be rid of those memories, no matter how far he drives.

The Projectionist's Daughter

Back in 1962, Providence, North Carolina, was typical of America's small towns. Main Street comprised a simple lineup that included a movie theater, barbershop, police station, and dime store. The Esso station could be found on the western end of the main drag, but at the eastern boundary of the town proper, where the line of commercial buildings gave way abruptly to the wide fields of the county's many tobacco farms, stood Doyle's Diner, a familiar gathering place of Providence's residents for decades.

The diner's owners were Billy Doyle—a tall, lanky man standing at six foot seven and considered by many to be the tallest man in the county, who'd taken over when his parents were killed in a car crash during his senior year of high school—and Billy's wife, Virginia, his sole waitress in those early years. Virginia was bookish and plain-looking—she was stout and had poor eyesight that forced her to wear thick-lensed glasses—and she took care of most of the business side of things. But Virginia was the apple of Billy Doyle's eye. Their sole employee at that time was one of Billy's former basketball teammates at Randolph High, a burly kid named Delmar who was the first post-segregation black student to attend their school.

In a stroke of good fortune, a year after Billy took ownership of Doyle's Diner, the state of North Carolina announced plans to begin construction on a stretch of interstate highway that would pass just south of Providence. Less than two years later the diner became a popular spot for cross-state travelers to interrupt their journeys for a rest and a meal. Business was so good, in fact, that Billy and Virginia were forced to hire a part-time employee to help out, the teenage daughter of the projectionist from the town's movie theater. Despite their good fortune, Billy told Virginia often that he worried it would all come crashing down around them one day, at which Virginia would shake her head and kiss his cheek.

"You are such a worrywart," she'd say.

"Why should we be so lucky when others have such a hard time?"

She'd always answer, "It's God's will."

Then came the miscarriages and Billy did not hear any more from his wife about God's will. Having children was the one topic the normally talkative Virginia refused to speak about. Billy would sometimes walk into their bedroom to find his wife lying facedown across the bed or sitting at her vanity, her cheeks damp from crying. At these times, he would back out of the room as quietly as possible and wait downstairs for her to appear. She would look at Billy, her eyes dry but still red, and give him a taut smile. He'd try to reassure her that things weren't so bad. He was pretty sure he never succeeded.

The girl who worked on weekends, the projectionist's daughter, was named Nancy. She was, certainly to Billy's mind, an extraordinary beauty. She had soft waves of deep auburn hair that seemed to shift color when she turned her head, and bright hazel eyes that were difficult not to stare at (for men at least). Much to Billy's chagrin, whenever Nancy worked at Doyle's Diner, there were always men flirting with the girl or making passes at her. It was also common for a half dozen boys to be loitering on the stools, nursing bottles of Cheerwine and unsuccessfully trying to hide their furtive leers. Billy, who was only about five years older than most of these boys, felt protective of Nancy and would come out from the kitchen every so often to warn the boys to be gentlemen while in his establishment. The boys and Nancy would giggle when he did this. Virginia would smile at her husband and then turn to give the boys a quick wink to let them know Billy's bark was infinitely worse than his bite.

After closing time on the weekends that Nancy worked, Billy would insist on walking her home. Her family lived just south of town in an isolated, run-down neighborhood that was situated behind the row of businesses on Main Street. Separating the movie theater and the Five and Dime was an alleyway that provided a shortcut to the cluster of streets where Nancy and her parents lived. On most nights when Billy would escort her home, they would walk in silence until turning into the alley where, the awkward silence becoming too much for her, Nancy would attempt to draw the taciturn fry cook into conversation.

"Have you ever met anyone taller than you?" Nancy asked one night.

"Not yet."

Billy told Nancy that it wasn't always an advantage being so much taller than most people. Buying clothes that fit was difficult, especially shoes. He'd have to drive to Winston-Salem or even Greensboro if he needed anything.

"Well, there has got to be more pluses than minuses to being tall."

"At a parade, I guess," Billy said after a moment, feeling the need to say something in reply.

"You think I'm pretty, don't you?" she asked one night, catching Billy off guard during their walk to her house.

He said that he did and quickly added that everyone he knew did as well.

"Prettier than your wife?"

He looked down at her and her eyes held his. Billy felt his cheeks burn.

"A husband can never think there's anyone prettier than his wife," Billy said.

He was pleased with his response and hoped that would be the end of the conversation, but she reached over and slid her tiny hand inside his, squeezing lightly.

"Your secret's safe with me," she said before pulling her hand away.

Billy could feel his cheeks flush and started to say something else, felt he should, but he just looked at her smiling at him and in that instant his silence betrayed his feelings.

When they reached Nancy's house that night, Billy stopped on the sidewalk to watch her until she disappeared through her front door, which was their routine. But this time, Nancy walked around in front of him and, standing on tiptoe, kissed him lightly on his lips before skipping along the walkway and up the front steps of the house. Then, just before pushing open the door, Nancy turned and gave a dramatic curtsy and waved. Despite the shock of the unexpected kiss, this caused Billy to smile.

A couple months later, on the Saturday before Thanksgiving, the weather turned unseasonably frigid and carried the rare threat of snow. The diner was busier than usual with flocks of people coming in to escape the cold. Billy bustled about the kitchen preparing orders. Behind him, Delmar whistled amid the clatter of the freshly rinsed dishes he was stacking next to the sink. From the dining area, Billy could hear the comforting din of dozens of conversations interspersed with Virginia's voice periodically shouting out orders. Every now and then, when Billy saw that Virginia wasn't looking, he'd peek out through the pass-through to watch Nancy clearing plates and refilling coffee cups, recalling how soft her hand felt against his own rough palm. And how soft her lips felt when she'd surprised him with a kiss.

A group of five boys Billy had never seen before were crowded into one of the corner booths, smoking, laughing loudly, and horsing around. Several of the boys wore letterman jackets from a high school in the adjoining county. Billy noticed whenever Nancy came near, they'd ask her to bring them a new straw or spoon or another order of fries or a refill of their Pepsi Colas. One of these boys, a tall swarthy kid with a thick neck and slicked hair, would try to pull her into the booth when she brought whatever they'd asked for. She would implore them to stop, warning them she'd get in trouble if they didn't, pushing away from their grasps, but smiling all the while. When she came into the kitchen to bring some dirty dishes to Delmar, Billy informed her that he was going to kick the boys out.

"They're just fooling around," Nancy said. "They don't mean any harm."

Billy told Nancy to just steer clear of them since it was getting late and they'd be closing soon. When the boys' final order of french fries was ready, Billy carried it over to their table himself.

"Here you go, fellas," Billy said. "Enjoy the fries. And, by the way. . .don't let me catch you in here ever again."

"Yeah? What're you gonna do about it?" the thick-necked boy asked.

"Do us all a favor and let's not find out, OK? Now eat up and get out of my diner."

After the diner closed and they were all cleaning up, Billy went to clear the booth where the boys had been sitting and noticed that one of them had written "FUCK YOU DOYLE" on the tabletop with the squeeze-bottle of ketchup. He wiped up the mess and never mentioned it to Virginia.

A couple weeks later, on their walk from the diner to her house, Nancy and Billy didn't talk, both of them seemingly lost in their own thoughts. Several times Billy noticed Nancy looking up at him, appearing upset and on the verge of saying something, but then she'd look away. That evening Billy watched Nancy hurry inside the house with no more than a mumbled good night. She didn't curtsy or wave or look back, but Billy had waved even after she'd shut the door. He stood with his hands stuffed in his trouser pockets, watching the house for several minutes before heading back toward his own house and his waiting wife.

At five-thirty the following morning, as Billy and Virginia were preparing the diner for the Sunday breakfast crowd, there was a loud knock on the diner's front door. Through the glass, Billy saw Walt Castle, one of Providence's three police officers. Billy noticed an unusually serious expression on the typically jovial policeman's face. Puffs of steam pulsed from Walt's nostrils in the frigid morning air. After Billy let him in and offered him a cup of coffee, Walt explained that Nancy's father had called the police station an hour earlier to report that Nancy was missing. She hadn't come home after work the previous night, the father had said, so Walt was starting his investigation at the last place she had been seen.

Billy explained how he'd walked Nancy home and watched her go into the house. When Walt asked if she'd seemed worried or troubled in any way, Billy thought about how quiet she had been and how she had rushed into the house without saying anything other than a muttered good night, but he answered that she seemed pretty normal to him. Walt wrote notes on a small pad with a stubby pencil.

"So you were the last person to see her alive," Walt said.

"She's dead?" Billy asked, an icy feeling seizing his gut.

"Poor choice of words. We don't know that. But you *were* the last person to see her, right?"

"I don't know. I suppose so."

"Oh, her poor parents," Virginia said, coming up beside Billy.

Walt nodded and wrote something else on his notepad. Billy wondered if he was writing "poor parents." Then the policeman asked if either Billy or Virginia could think of anyone else who might help him find the missing girl. The Doyles shook their heads in unison. Walt drained his coffee cup, thanked them, and turned to leave. Just then, Billy remembered the rowdy group of boys in the corner booth. He told Walt about them, describing as many as he could remember, especially the boy with the slicked hair who'd grabbed Nancy. Virginia occasionally corrected some detail. Billy indicated that they wore high school letterman jackets from the adjacent county and added that he thought they'd been drinking beer. When Walt finished his notes and left, Billy relocked the door behind him even though it was only fifteen minutes until the diner opened for business.

"Why did you say that? About those boys drinking?" Virginia asked when Walt was pulling away in his patrol car.

"Boys that age, it's very possible," he said. "Heck, even likely. You know that."

The truth was he wasn't sure why he'd said it, but even as Virginia headed back to the kitchen, Billy stood there, picturing Nancy curtsying and waving goodbye.

The Sunday after-church crowd was twice as large as usual; the whole town, it seemed, had gathered at Doyle's Diner to discuss the news of the missing girl, which had spread like a contagion. The prevailing theory was that she'd run off with a boy, but there were plenty who suspected foul play by the antisocial projectionist or his wife. Billy considered the latter just the nonsensical ranting of mean-spirited people and the former unlikely. As pretty as she was, Nancy never talked about boys, and she didn't have a steady boyfriend.

Walt Castle dropped by the diner twice more during the week following Nancy's disappearance in order to clarify some points in Billy's initial statement. Walt told him that he'd checked out the boys from Davidson County; all had solid alibis for where they'd been after leaving the diner the night of Nancy's disappearance. The last public sighting of the girl, the policeman said, was by a couple who, while waiting outside the movie theater for friends, had seen Billy and Nancy turn into the alley.

"Technically, *I* made the last sighting," Billy said, a bit more testily than he'd intended.

Walt looked at him and Billy could see that the policeman was someone who didn't like to be corrected.

"Well, if you'll excuse me, I'm kind of busy," Billy said, even though there was only one customer in the diner.

After Walt Castle left, Billy was sullen for the rest of the day. He asked Delmar to please stop his incessant whistling, and once when Virginia leaned through the pass-through window to ask if an order was ready, he snapped at her—something he'd never done before.

"You're acting meaner than a sore-tailed cat, Billy Doyle," she said at home that night. She was packing up some fried chicken and a pecan pie to take over to Nancy's family. "What's eating at you?"

"Walt Castle thinks I might have something to do with Nancy going missing."

"That's nonsense. He thinks no such thing."

"Is it? You didn't see how he looked at me today. And why does he keep wasting time coming around to talk to me instead of being out there looking for that poor girl?"

"He's probably hit a dead end," she said. "The police must be under a lot of pressure."

He conceded that might be true, but Billy couldn't shake the feeling he was a suspect.

"Come with me to deliver this food," Virginia said. "The walk'll do you good."

They hadn't saved enough money for a car yet, so the Doyles walked arm in arm through the crisp autumn evening. When they came to Main Street, both of them stopped to look up at the darkened marquee of the movie theater, which had been closed ever since Nancy's disappearance. Billy started to walk toward the west end of the block, but his wife pulled him in the opposite direction.

"Where're you going?" she said. "Let's cut through the alleyway. It's faster."

Billy hesitated.

"What's wrong?" Virginia asked.

"Nothing. Just hadn't thought about cutting through the alley is all."

Of course, Billy *had* thought about the alley. He just didn't want to be reminded of all the times he and Nancy passed through it together, especially their last time. Or how nice it felt the time she'd held his hand and kissed him. When Billy and Virginia crossed through the alley and emerged two blocks from the projectionist's house, Billy wondered if he should have told Virginia about what had happened that night. He glanced down at his wife, who was staring at him with an odd look on her face.

"Is something bothering you, Billy?" she asked.

"No. I'm fine. Why do you say that?"

"You look distressed all of a sudden. And you've been acting strange ever since we left the house."

"I'm okay. Let's hurry now. It's getting chilly."

When they reached Nancy's house, Billy stood to the side of the door and held the basket containing the chicken and the pie while Virginia opened the screen door and knocked. For a moment, he thought no one was going to answer and actually hoped that was so, but then the heavy oak door swung open, its hinges squeaking softly.

The projectionist was a short, stooped man with the pale skin of someone who spent the majority of the time in the dark. Like most of Providence's citizens, Billy did not know the reclusive man well—rarely did Billy and Virginia go to the movies and Nancy's father had been in the diner only once—but it seemed to Billy the man had aged considerably in the past week. The projectionist looked at them in turn with an expression Billy found unreadable.

"Yes?"

"We hope we're not disturbing you and your wife," Virginia said. "We know that these have been difficult days for you both and we wanted to bring you a little something, just to help out."

She gestured toward Billy, who took his cue to hand the basket to the man.

"Just some chicken, and a pie for dessert," Virginia added. "It must be hard for your wife to think about cooking."

The projectionist looked at Virginia and said nothing, his blank expression unchanged. He turned toward her husband, looking first at the food basket and then up at Billy's face. Being short, he had to bend his neck back a good ways to do this. And then Billy saw a shift in the man's eyes, like a sudden recognition, and his brows began to furrow.

"You're the diner fella, ain't you?" the projectionist said.

"Yes, sir. Name's Billy Doyle."

"You was with my baby girl when she went missin'?"

"No, sir. I walked her home to make sure she was safe and—"

"Don't you lie to me! I seen you two kissing."

Billy experienced a sudden sensation as though all the air had been squeezed from his body. He stared at the older man, unable to speak. Billy peeked at Virginia. She was looking right at him, her eyes wide and her mouth dropped open.

"You got some kind of nerve showing your face around here," the projectionist shouted, a mizzle of spit spraying out with the words. "I told Walt Castle that you ought to be drug into the police station and beaten until you tell what you done to my girl."

The projectionist's face, neck, and cheeks flushed deep red and his eyes widened, his pupils dilating like a feral animal. He took a step toward Billy, who lifted his arm to ward off a blow, but instead the man slapped the basket out of Billy's hands, sending its contents bouncing and rolling across the chipped, uneven boards of the porch.

"Get the hell out of here! If I see you again, I'll shoot you as sure as you're standing here."

"Sir, please," Virginia started, "surely there's some kind of mistake. . ." but the man turned toward her and when she saw the fury in his eyes, she flinched.

"Get off my property before I call the police. And take your pissant peace offering with you."

Billy and Virginia gathered up the dirt-flecked pieces of fried chicken and scooped globs of spilled pecan pie into the basket and hurried off the porch. Billy wrapped his arm around his wife, pulling her tight against him, and they walked home in silence. Tears ran down Virginia's face, but she made no move to wipe them away.

Once home, Billy poured them each a small glass of brandy from a dusty bottle he kept hidden on the back of the pantry's top shelf. Virginia rarely drank alcohol, but she accepted the glass readily when Billy proffered it. When she stopped crying, Billy came over to the sofa and sat down beside her.

"Why would he say that, Billy? About you kissing his daughter?"

Billy sensed his neck and cheeks reddening. He leaned

toward the small coffee table where the bottle of brandy was and refilled his glass so his wife couldn't see his face. He drank most of what he had just poured in one big swallow and sat back. He turned toward Virginia, who was waiting for him to explain. He'd never lied to his wife, never needed to; Billy realized he was, at that moment, at an important crossroads in his marriage.

"I don't know," he said at last. "He must be mistaking me for someone else he saw kissing Nancy."

Virginia held her husband's eyes for what seemed like an eternity to him, then took a sip from her glass.

"That explains one thing," Billy said. "Now we know why Walt Castle keeps coming back to the diner. Nancy's father has been putting foolish ideas into his head."

Again Virginia studied Billy's eyes. At last, she leaned forward and poured herself another glass of brandy, filling it nearly to the point of overflowing.

While it had been their routine ever since getting married to walk to the diner together in the early morning hours no matter the weather—when the streets of Providence were hushed and tranquil—the following morning Virginia told Billy to go on ahead to work, that she had a couple errands to run and would meet him before opening. Billy was surprised by his wife's statement. She'd never mentioned any errands to him and he suspected there truly weren't any, but he didn't argue the point. He knew she was still upset about the events of the prior evening. But over the next several days, Virginia made other excuses to avoid walking to work with Billy and it quickly became evident they'd begun a new routine. After a month, Billy stopped asking Virginia each morning if she was coming with him. And while Billy Doyle was no master of subtlety, he understood that ever since Nancy's father had said he'd seen Billy kissing his daughter, his marriage was, for the first time, in real danger.

Billy would remind himself that he hadn't done anything wrong. Many times he would stand sweating over the griddle at the diner, trying to infuse in himself a sense of outrage at being misjudged. But this thought was usually splintered by guilt-ridden memories of how soft Nancy's hand felt in his, or how warm her lips had been when she'd kissed him. Billy knew he had nothing to do with the girl's disappearance, so he mostly found himself wishing Nancy would simply show up. Not so much for everyone to know she was safe, but so that she could clear things up for his wife.

But five months later, Nancy's whereabouts still remained unknown. Initially, the girl's disappearance had incited a flurry of interest from newspapers as far away as Charlotte and Richmond, but as spring approached, the matter once again became Providence's own private mystery. And the uneasiness surrounding the case had seeped deep into the town's collective psyche. Rumors spread that Billy and Nancy "had a thing" and that was why she had to go away. Billy noticed that certain regulars no longer patronized the diner, and Delmar confirmed that some members of his church's congregation had been whispering about it when they thought Delmar was out of earshot.

Even with the loss of some local customers, business at the diner continued to be brisk thanks to the increased traffic on the new interstate highway. Without Nancy to help, Virginia was forced to handle all the waitressing duties by herself. Billy was uncomfortable with the idea of replacing the girl, almost to the point of superstition. Besides, the days seemed easier when he and his wife didn't have time to think about anything but work. They never spoke about Nancy or about their visit to the projectionist's house, but the girl's aura seemed to pervade their lives like an invisible and disquieting fog that never lifted. Worst of all, Billy secretly despaired that his wife had stopped loving him.

Then one bright May morning, as the breakfast rush subsided, Walt Castle walked in the diner and asked Billy and Virginia if they'd heard the news.

"What news would that be?" Virginia asked cooly as she wiped toast crumbs off the countertop with a damp cloth.

"Nancy's back in town."

"When? How?" Billy asked, leaning across the pass-through.

Several of the lingering patrons, most of them locals, turned to listen to what the policeman had to say.

"I'm not at liberty to divulge details," Walt said, "but it turns out she's been in Raleigh all this time. At a hospital a good part of it."

"Oh, my," Virginia said. "What happened?"

Walt looked about the diner and kicked lightly at something on the floor with the toe of one shiny Brogue, and Billy surmised the policeman regretted saying as much as he had.

"Well," Walt said, pausing momentarily as if to weigh his words carefully, "a good bit of it was written about in the Raleigh papers, so it's not exactly a secret. There was a nurse arrested. Nancy was not her first by a long shot, from what I hear. Poor girl. Apparently they found Nancy just in time, before she bled to death."

Billy looked at Virginia, who had put her hand up to her mouth in surprise, and he saw that she understood something he did not. But he sensed it was not the time to ask about it. After a couple minutes of awkward silence, Walt said goodbye and left. An animated murmur rose from the booths of customers, more than a few of whom stole looks at Billy.

As they went about the business of the day, preparing first for lunch and then dinner, Billy and Virginia said nothing to each other about Walt Castle's visit or the news he'd brought. Billy pondered what it was that had happened to Nancy, but a big part of him understood he didn't want to know. Now and then, as he scraped charred bits of burger meat and grease off the griddle, or lowered baskets of french fries into the sizzling fryer, he thought of the last time he'd seen the girl. She had seemed distracted and upset, obviously wanting to tell him something. He should have spoken first and encouraged her to open up to him. Would that have changed anything? All day, he desperately wanted to talk with Virginia about it, but he waited for her to bring it up first. She never did.

Within a few weeks of the news of Nancy's return, the projectionist moved his family up north and Billy never heard of them again. More details had emerged about Nancy's disappearance. The nurse who'd been arrested hanged herself in her prison cell the night before her trial was set to begin, and there was new information about a traveling salesman almost twenty years older than Nancy who the police were actively searching for. The amount of tawdry buzz that pervaded Providence during those days had not been seen before or since.

Eventually Billy hired another waitress, a widow friend of Virginia's who'd lost her husband suddenly to a heart attack at the age of forty-eight, and life at Doyle's Diner returned to a monotonous, comforting routine.

One evening at home, Billy wandered into their bedroom to find Virginia smoothing the corner of a bedsheet she'd just put on. Not long after they'd learned about Nancy's return and her problem, Virginia had gotten into the habit of changing the sheets every night before they retired, something Billy found odd and disquieting. He had learned to stop questioning, though, because Virginia's answer to why she did it was always that she simply felt like it. Without speaking, he walked over and took hold of one edge of the spread and helped her align it. They had not been intimate in months and Billy yearned to hold his wife in bed. When they'd finished with the bed linen, Virginia folded down the sheet in preparation for retiring, then walked into the bathroom. Billy heard the water running into the bathtub as she readied her bath. He called her name.

She didn't answer. Billy hoped it was only because of the noise from the rushing water. A brief sense of desperation flickered inside him like a nervous tickle in his midsection. The water stopped. "Virginia," he said, and waited.

She appeared at the bathroom door, clutching her robe closed with her hands.

"Do you love me?" he asked.

"Oh, for God's sake, William Doyle. You ask the stupidest questions." She let one hand go from the front of her robe and reached up to remove the bobby pins from her hair bun. She shook her head once, letting strands of hair fall over her shoulders, and disappeared back into the bathroom. After a minute, Billy could hear the soft splash as she slid into the water.

Although she was out of view, Billy nodded. He often felt stupid around her, but not just when he asked her questions. And, more importantly, he realized, he didn't feel *just* stupid; he felt guilty. How could he ever tell Virginia of the nugget of shame he felt whenever he thought about Nancy? The shame that he knew had nothing to do with what happened to the girl, but rather with the pleasantness he felt whenever he recalled that one time she had kissed him. He pushed that thought to the back of his mind and convinced himself, as he always did, that it was a frivolous and innocent memory. After all, it truly was.

Billy undressed and climbed into bed to wait for his wife to join him. After she did, he turned onto his side and reached over, placing his hand on her arm. To his surprise, she didn't pull it away. Billy wanted to say something then, something healing or clever, but his mind could not fix on anything.

"I heard there's a new Italian restaurant in Winston-Salem," he said at last. "Would you like to go this Saturday night? We haven't dressed up and gone out in a long time."

Virginia craned her head back to look at him before placing her free hand on top his own, which still rested on her arm.

"That would be lovely," she said, and smiled.

It was the first smile he'd seen on his wife's face in a very long while, and it filled Billy Doyle with hope.

Ripples

One bright, temperate afternoon in April that arrived like serendipity following an unusually long winter, Guy Monroe, one of Forsyth County's most respected gastroenterologists, injected his sleeping three-year-old son with a fatal overdose of potassium chloride, then shot himself in the head.

Five days prior, Guy and his wife had received news that their son's glioblastoma, a particularly aggressive form of brain tumor, had stopped responding to treatment and had spread widely to the adjacent tissues of the brain. The tumor, discovered not long before Liam's first birthday, had been held in check for over two years only by aggressive treatments that included surgery and radiation combined with multi-drug therapies, heartrending things for parents to watch. As a medical doctor himself, Guy knew exactly what this latest news meant. With luck, their son might live two or three agonizing weeks. But luck was not something he or Kathleen seemed to possess.

The day he did it, Guy had sent his wife to Walgreen's to pick up a refill of Liam's pain medication. He'd insisted she go because, he told her, he had to stay and check the patency of the injection port the nurses had placed in Liam's neck prior to his most recent round of chemo. Guy also explained he could see that the burden of looking after their son was taking a toll on her. Even thirty minutes out of the house would be beneficial for her, especially on such a pleasant day.

And so, one day after Guy had walked into a local gun shop to buy a revolver he told the clerk he needed after a break-in at their house, he kissed Kathleen and assured her that he had everything under control before watching her drive off to pick up a prescription that didn't exist.

Kathleen listened as her husband's phone transferred to voicemail for the second time and felt anger and frustration building inside her. They'd made a rule—one Guy himself had insisted upon ever since Liam's diagnosis—that they would answer their phones no matter what else they were doing. So not only was there some confusion at the pharmacy about their son's prescription not being on file, Guy was ignoring his own ironclad policy for the first time. Yet by the time Kathleen pulled the Volvo into their driveway, fear had replaced her anger. On the drive home she'd redialed her husband's phone five times, each call ending with his recorded voice directing her to leave a message. And while seeing Guy's car parked in front of the garage relieved a small portion of that fear, nothing could have prepared her for the scene she was about to discover.

Later, thinking back on the moment she had walked into the house, Kathleen would not be able to say if it was the smell or the quiet that had unnerved her more. She didn't recognize the odor, never having fired a gun or been around anyone who had. It was faint at first but grew stronger as she climbed the steps to the bedrooms, all the while calling Guy's name over and over, the volume of her voice rising in concert with her panic.

When she pushed open the door to Liam's room, a thin haze of smoke hovered near the ceiling and the air was thick with the burnt-egg smell of the discharged gun. It was strong and nauseating, but she didn't vomit. Not until she saw them.

In a city the size of Winston-Salem, a scene like the one at the Monroe home wasn't kept under wraps for long. Within an hour of the arrival of the first police cruiser (three more, as well as two ambulances, came not long after), a crowd of neighbors and news vans packed the typically quiet street in what was arguably the most affluent area of town.

The first officer on the scene, who happened to be driving nearby when Kathleen's call came in to 911, was new on the job, having graduated the academy only seven months prior. After surveying the devastation in Liam Monroe's bedroom, he sat silently with Kathleen downstairs on the sofa in the living room until backup arrived. A policewoman relieved him so he could talk to the detectives. After giving what few details he knew, the young cop offered to cordon off the house outside, mostly because he was shaky and he didn't want the older cops to see him cry. The officer's mother had told him frequently that she thought he was too sensitive a boy to have a job that involved such brutal things. The irony was that his desire to become a cop was in large part tied to wanting to prove her wrong.

Kathleen Monroe's sister, who lived a little more than an hour away, just north of the Virginia line, was summoned to come help. While they waited for her arrival, Didi Patton, the young policewoman who sat consoling Mrs. Monroe in the living room, put her arm around the woman's shoulder and held her against her chest until Kathleen's sobbing slowed. Didi could tell that the woman's face was pressed against her service badge but Mrs. Monroe gave no indication she felt it or was bothered by it. There were no words, Didi knew, that would ease the pain of this woman's shock and sorrow, at least not this soon, so she simply held her and let her weep.

The policewoman scanned the room, observing it in a methodical, sweeping arc, a habit she'd acquired on the job. The house was large and beautiful, the living room immaculately kept and decorated with furnishings Didi knew likely cost more than she'd make in several years as a cop. She'd grown up in a working-class household—her father was a welder and her mother a part-time waitress at the Waffle House—and although her parents had provided for her and her brother well enough, she'd always felt uneasy when friends came to her house for the first time. Their furniture was clean and functional but seemed to Didi always just past its useful lifespan, with tattered edges and worn spots in the upholstery. The only time she'd been invited into a home as expensive and nice as this one was on official business. And while she'd learned in just a handful of years on the force that you can never judge people by how much money or success they had, she still found it bewildering that someone who seemed to have everything could reach the point where he'd murder his own child, kill himself, and leave the wife he loved all alone.

Contemplating the end of Mrs. Monroe's marriage, an event that occurred literally less than an hour before, brought up thoughts about her own upcoming wedding. Didi was engaged to a fellow officer. They'd met on the first day of training and began dating soon after graduating from the academy. That very morning, before heading in to work, she'd been on the phone with her mother discussing options for wedding flowers. Didi remembered how excited her mother sounded. And how happy she herself felt at the idea of being married. But looking down at the top of Kathleen Monroe's head pressed against her chest, close enough to smell the bergamot scent in her hair, Didi felt a discomfiting prickle that she tried to ignore, but couldn't.

When the paramedics navigated the first stretcher down the stairs, the clatter of the metal legs and wheels startled Mrs. Monroe, and she sat up abruptly. Didi patted the woman's shoulders and did her best to shield Kathleen's view as the stretcher passed on the way to the front door, but in the end they both silently watched as her baby's shrouded body rolled into, and out of, view.

When Kathleen's sister, Lucy, got the call from Officer Patton of the Winston-Salem Police Department, she was at the Mill Mountain Zoo in Roanoke, standing in front of an outdoor enclosure containing a Eurasian Lynx. She was one of three parents chaperoning a group of second and third graders from her daughter's school. When her phone had rung, she'd meant to simply silence it, but when she saw it was a Winston-Salem-area number she didn't recognize, curiosity convinced her to answer it. The policewoman on the other end had explained only that Lucy's brother-in-law and nephew had died and requested she come down to be with her sister as soon as possible.

Lucy stood trembling, suddenly cold. The children and other adults had moved away, down the path that would take them to the otter exhibit, and when she looked up she noticed the lynx crouching on a thick branch, staring at her. The controlled menace in the cat's eyes sent a chill through her and she hurried to catch up to the group. She pulled one of the other parents aside to explain her situation and to ask if they'd take Lucy's daughter home with them until her father could pick her up after work. Lucy then explained to her daughter that she had to go visit Aunt Kathleen right away, but hopefully she'd be back the next day. She looked into her daughter's young, naïve eyes, fighting to hold back the imminent flood of tears, and an image of Liam lying silent and pale on a morgue table flashed across her mind. She was seized by an urge to grab her daughter and hold her. Lucy was reluctant to leave, as though her ankles were stuck in a pool of thick mud. Instead, she kissed her daughter quickly and hurried away to face whatever horror awaited in Winston-Salem.

Lauren Delaney, a registered nurse, was Guy Monroe's primary assistant at his gastroenterology practice. She sat ashen on her couch, watching the local news. Ten minutes before, she'd received a text from a friend who also worked at the practice informing her about Dr. Monroe's death. Too shocked to even cry, Lauren watched the TV screen showing paramedics wheeling two sheet-covered stretchers along the front walkway of a house she'd been inside many times. The camera followed the stretchers until they'd been loaded into separate ambulances. Lauren noticed there were no lights and no sirens as they pulled away and it was that, like a traffic light changing from red to green, which finally triggered her tears.

Details were lacking in the information the television reporter gave, but initial reports indicated there had been a murder-suicide involving Dr. Monroe and his son. That news sent a wave of panic-infused guilt through Lauren, a tingly heat that rose from deep inside of her and caused uncontrollable shivers. When the phone resting on her lap buzzed it startled her, causing her to jump enough to knock the phone onto the floor. Rattled and frightened, she scrambled to fetch it, terrified that she would see Guy's name and photo on the display even though she knew that was impossible.

She leaned over to retrieve the phone but stopped halfway, her outstretched hand hovering above it as if she'd suddenly decided to bless the device rather than pick it up.

The phone buzzed and buzzed but soon stopped as the call switched over to voicemail. She stared at it for a long while, as the guilt that had filled her moments before was replaced by fear, a fear fueled by an unbidden flurry of questions: *Where is Guy's phone, and who has it? Has he saved any of the photos or emails I sent him? Will Kathleen somehow be given access to them now?*

She scooped the phone off the carpet and squeezed it tightly in her palm, momentarily contemplating hurling it against the wall. Instead, she unlocked it and began deleting everything she'd received from Guy since the beginning of their affair.

In the days immediately after, the calamity of the Monroe family was the big story in the Triad area. Guy had left no note, no explicit explanation as to why he had done what he did. Those who knew him best—his friends, his patients, coworkers—all said Guy was the finest sort of person, selfless and kind. He'd never shown signs that he was capable of such a dreadful act, but everyone agreed: wasn't that the way it always was with these things? You could never know what lurked deep in a man's soul, after all.

Around town many theories about marriage difficulties or undiagnosed mental illness were bandied about, but most people, including the detectives assigned to the case, ultimately agreed that what had occurred had been a desperate father's desire to end his beloved son's inescapable suffering—a simple, if misguided, attempt at humane euthanasia—as well as a desire to spare his wife the agony of the criminal trial that would have surely ensued. But one conclusion seemed inescapable: the community had lost one of its best and brightest.

In a chilly laboratory on the lowest level of Baptist Hospital, Carin Oberlin pressed buttons on the analyzer into which she'd just placed the second sample of Liam Monroe's blood. As Deputy Chief Toxicologist for Forsyth County, she'd been tasked with confirming the cause of the boy's death. A syringe found on the nightstand next to Liam's bed had already been determined to contain potassium chloride, so it was assumed his father, with his medical knowledge, had used it to end his son's life. And sure enough, the first sample tested had shown extremely high levels of the compound in Liam's blood, hundreds of times the level used therapeutically for treating low potassium in patients. Per standard operating procedure, Carin always repeated toxicology tests with such abnormal results and, within minutes, the computer had confirmed the initial testing. Three-year-old Liam Monroe had been killed, beyond doubt, by an overdose of the drug.

As a toxicologist, Carin had many times over the years had discussions with her colleagues, usually at bars or parties after a few drinks, regarding which toxin would be the best to use as a murder weapon. The debate always centered on finding something that was undetectable on tox tests. Potassium chloride was never considered because it was so easy to screen for, but she knew that Guy Monroe, in any event, was not trying to conceal his crime. He wanted only to get the job done.

Many, if not most, in the Winston-Salem area and beyond, who had heard about how Guy Monroe ended his baby son's life, considered Guy a monster. But when Carin stared at the printout showing the extreme value of potassium in Liam's blood she couldn't help but wonder if the inordinate amount of courage it took to push the plunger on the syringe, an act that likely took close to a minute considering how much drug would have been needed to account for the levels she detected, actually made Guy Monroe in some way better than everyone else. Could she, she pondered, ever love someone so much that she could do what Monroe had done?

She slid the toxicology report into a folder and headed off to her desk to finalize her notes to send to the Medical Examiner's office. Glancing at the clock above the lab's door she told herself that if she hurried she could still meet her boyfriend for lunch.

The Monroe's house itself became briefly famous for a time right after the deaths. It was a rare thing for such mayhem to occur in one of the city's well-heeled areas. Cars would drive by and slow down, passengers gawking, hoping to see some outward vestige of the horror that had occurred inside to titillate them and liven up their boring lives. Some would go so far as to park and walk onto the front lawn to snap selfies in front of the house. At first, the neighbors—acquaintances of Guy and Kathleen Monroe—would shoo the rubberneckers away and reprimand them for being disrespectful. But within weeks, the novelty wore off and both the curiosity seekers and the neighbors alike ignored the empty home with the shiny, new For Sale sign.

As the first anniversary of the tragedy approached, Kathleen Monroe sat in her sister's living room, sipping a cup of tea. Following the settlement of their estate, she'd moved up to Virginia to be near her only remaining family. She'd even renewed her nurse's license and was now working at a local hospital. She was still young and attractive, so it was no surprise when one of the surgeons at the hospital had asked her on dates several times. Contrary to her sister's advice, Kathleen had refused every time. She wasn't ready for a relationship yet. Even months and months of counseling had not abated the deep well of anger she harbored against her husband.

"Your being angry isn't going to bring them back, Kat," her sister said. "You've got to let it go."

"Don't you think I know that? I try, but I can't. Aren't you mad, too?"

"Of course I am."

"It didn't have to happen," Kathleen said softly, more to herself than to her sister. "Even if we knew we had to lose Liam, Guy should still be here."

Kathleen's niece, who was playing quietly in the adjacent room, listened to the conversation between the adults. No one had told her specifically what had happened to her uncle and cousin that day, but she'd heard enough at the time of the funerals to understand that Uncle Guy had made Liam die and then made himself die. All the grown-ups kept saying they didn't understand why he did it.

But she did. It was obvious. Uncle Guy knew that if Liam got to heaven all by himself, without his mommy or daddy, he would be really scared. He would be like the lynx they saw at the zoo that day. The big cat's eyes looked so scared and sad as he sat all alone in his tree, surrounded by strangers staring at him, with no family or friends with him. Liam would have been like that. She was glad he didn't have to go up to heaven alone, and she was happy that when her time came, Liam and Uncle Guy would already be there waiting to welcome her. To welcome all of them.

Poke

I race to the edge of the woods and wait for Poke. His real name is Austin, but no one ever calls him that, except his mom. But the nickname fits. He's the slowest kid I've ever known. I realize it's just because he's so fat, and most of the time his slowness doesn't bother me, but I'm anxious to check out what Connor told us about at school today. He'd said it was the coolest (which to Connor meant "grossest") thing he'd ever seen. Connor made Poke and me promise not to say anything to anyone about it. Especially grown-ups.

Poke is wheezing hard when he catches up. A huge drop of sweat slides down his temple. His slick, red-orange hair practically glows when the sun hits it.

"Do you think Connor was bullshitting us?" Poke says after he catches his breath.

I glance into the dark woods, the smell of the much cooler, pine-scented air feeling almost like a warning. A small part of me hopes Connor *was* lying.

"I don't know, Poke. But there's one way to find out."

"Hold on a sec." Poke digs into a pocket of his jeans and pulls out a shiny coin. It's a silver dollar from the year he was born that his dad had given him a long time ago for his birthday. Poke carries it around with him everywhere, pulling it out to rub it for luck when he thinks he needs some. I watch him close his eyes and run his thumb in a circle over the coin.

"OK, let's go," he says.

When we start onto the well-worn path into the patch of trees behind our school we no longer hurry. The woods aren't all that big, but they're large enough for people to do stuff without being seen or heard. Most of the kids we know come here on weekends to mess around—the younger ones to play army or hide-and-seek, the teenagers to drink or smoke or make out—and normally it's not scary, but as Poke and I follow the path around a sharp bend, losing sight of the entrance, I have to confess to feeling a bit nervous. Every time we hear a sound we both stop and stare in its direction.

"This is stupid," Poke says, and I can tell he's jittery, too. "Connor was just messing with us. My mom's gonna start wondering where I am."

Mrs. Fitzgerald is the most overprotective parent I know. Poke's dad left her eight years ago, when Poke was five, so she's always saying that Austin is the only thing she has left. He has to check in with her multiple times whenever he comes over to play at my house. I once overheard my parents talking about Poke's father and, although they didn't come right out and say it, I was old enough to understand that they think he ran off with another woman. And what made it worse was he took their dog, a Husky named Lucy that Poke loved a ton.

"Yeah, there's a good chance Connor's just screwing with us. I bet he's watching us, laughing his ass off. You and I both know there aren't any wolves around here. But if we leave now he'll never let us hear the end of it. Let's just get there so we can go home."

The place Connor told us about is in the densest area of the woods. He'd said to stand on top of Cougar Rock (so called because legend has it years ago a cougar wandered into town and dragged a small child from a backyard to bring back to this boulder to eat; but the likelihood of there being cougars here is about as probable as wolves roaming around). From up there we'd see a dead tree leaning at a forty-five-degree angle if we looked carefully through the trunks of the other trees. What we came looking for is at the base of that dead tree. Weaving our way between the trees, neither Poke nor I say anything. We're watching closely for anything that might surprise us. It's dark and cool, and when I look straight up the sky is nothing but a bunch of blue speckles dotting the tops of the leaves. I rub my arms to erase goosebumps, even though it's not that cold.

"There's the rock," I say as we reach the top of a small hill.

Poke tiptoes to look over my shoulder and nods. The top of Cougar Rock is at the level of my shoulders, but it has enough crannies to make it easy to climb. At the rock's base, cigarette butts and a crinkled Budweiser can litter the leaves and pine needles.

"Hang on," I say. "I'll go up and take a look."

I scramble up and stand in the boulder's flat center. Connor didn't tell us which direction to look, so I rotate slowly, my sneakers scuffing on the rough surface, craning my neck to get a good view into the woods. The fallen tree Connor mentioned is farther back than I expect and I nearly miss it. The trunk leans toward my left, snagged in the branches of nearby trees.

I point in its direction. "There it is."

I hop down and we head toward the fallen tree. Dry branches and pine needles crunch under our feet and the sound seems louder than usual. In my heart I know there's nothing to be afraid of, but I stop, turn back toward Poke, and press a finger against my lips. When we start again I make my steps as light as possible.

Once we reach the dead pine tree, I am amazed by its length, which I estimate is two to three times the width of my house.

"Connor said to look where the tree popped out of the ground," I say.

We follow the trunk, like an arrow pointing down to a prize, and just when we reach the large clod of dirt and roots at the end, a loud bell begins ringing. I jump. It takes me a second to recognize the ringtone from Poke's cell phone.

"Jesus, Poke, shut that thing off."

Poke fumbles in his pocket and pulls out the phone. "It's my mom. I knew she'd start getting worried."

"Text her and tell her you're staying at school to work on an extra-credit project for History class. You'll be home in thirty minutes. An hour tops."

"She won't buy it."

"Just try it, Poke."

I watch him tap out the message. He shakes his head while he waits for a reply. A ding sounds and he reads her answer.

"Holy shit, she believed me." Poke looks at me, a huge grin on his face. "She even said she was proud of me."

"Tell her thanks and then shut your ringer off."

Poke shoves the phone back into the pocket of his jeans.

I go and stand at the tree's base where a tangle of roots—some thick, some skinny—jut from a massive clump of dirt. Where the tree had popped out of the ground is a small crater. Tiny black bugs crawl around the hole, appearing and disappearing beneath the broken earth. All around the area the ground is torn up.

"Look around," I say. "Connor said he covered it up with a pile of leaves."

It doesn't take us long to find it. A few steps from where we're standing is a carefully arranged pile of leaves and pine needles that doesn't look like they fell that way naturally.

"That must be it," I say, walking over to take a closer look.

For a full minute Poke and I stare down, neither of us sure whether we want to see what's underneath. Finally, I start to push some of the leaves off with the toe of my sneaker.

"Help me," I say when Poke doesn't move.

"Forget it. This is stupid."

"For shit's sake, Poke, we've come all this way. Let's just see what it is."

Inspired by my own boldness, I increase the vigor with which I kick the leaves and needles off, and soon expose the dead animal's skull. Both of us jump back.

"Whoa. He wasn't lying," Poke says.

I recover from my initial shock and stare at the skull. It is tilted down, but even though I know they can't hurt me, the long snout and large, pointed teeth still look deadly. I scan the ground and notice a long stick lying a short distance away. I use it to brush off the remainder of the leaf pile concealing the bones. When I'm done we find ourselves gawking at an entire, intact wolf skeleton. Parts of some bones still have globs of dried skin and tissue clinging to them. Near the tail are small tufts of white and gray hair.

"Jeez, I guess there really are wolves around here," Poke whispers. His head swivels in both directions. "Do you think there are more, Drake?"

I consider the question. "I don't know, but we'd better cover this back up and get back." I take a quick look around, listening for anything moving in the woods. "Your mom *is* probably getting pretty worried about you."

We kick at the leaves, shoving them with the sides of our sneakers, trying to cover the bones, eventually bending down to scoop handfuls to toss over. Neither of us wants to get too close to the skeleton. When we figure we've hidden it enough (a few bones are still visible, but we're anxious to leave) we stand up and look at each other. A crackling sound comes from close by in the woods and I freeze. Poke jumps backward and when he does, the heel of his shoe catches and he falls hard. He scrambles to stand up, but when he pushes up with his hand, it sinks into the broken dirt. I see him roll away fast and jump up.

"There's something under there," he says, pointing down at where he'd fallen.

Sure enough, when I look at where he's indicating, something white is visible beneath the surface.

"Let's go, Drake," Poke says. "This is creeping me out, big time."

I stare at what Poke has exposed and I can't help but wonder if there's another wolf skeleton, and if we've stumbled onto an old, sacred Indian burial site, or something like it. Even though I'm scared too, I know that if we've found wolf bones of our own, it would impress Connor and the other older kids. I pick up the stick I'd tossed down. It doesn't take much scraping away of the dirt to see that there are, in fact, more bones there. But as I continue unearthing them, it becomes obvious these bones are bigger than the other wolf's.

"What are you doing?" Poke asks. "We need to get out of here."

"Look at this bone. It's way bigger!"

I continue uncovering a long, straight bone with my stick, following its length, until I see a gap. I keep rooting, exposing smaller bones now, and all at once I realize that what I am exposing is not a wolf's leg.

The bones that emerge are from a human hand.

I look at Poke, throw the stick away and run. I don't check behind me, but I can hear Poke wheezing as he struggles to keep up. Coming around a bend, I trip over a tree root and slam into the ground, and I lose my breath. I can hear Poke crashing through the woods not far off. After I recover, I jump up and continue running until I emerge into the bright sunlight, onto the field behind our school. I don't stop until I'm halfway across the grass. The sunshine and warmth of the air are comforting and I sense my heart rate easing up. I walk backward slowly, watching for Poke to appear. After what seems like ages, he stumbles out of the woods, holding his side. When he reaches me, his shirt has dark arcs at the armpits and his entire face is dotted with sweat. He bends over, resting his hands on his knees until he recovers enough to talk.

"What do we do now?" he asks.

"We can't tell anyone. We'll get in big trouble. You have to promise me you won't say a word to anybody, Poke.

"Do you think it's a pirate's body?" Poke asks.

I stare at him, trying to gauge if he's being serious. I conclude he is. "I doubt there were many pirates in Wilkesboro. Pirates hung around the ocean, not the mountains, idiot."

"I just thought there might be treasure there, too."

I start laughing, as much from the absurdity of Poke's comment as from the relief of being back in the daylight and safety of being near our school.

"We better get home," I say.

We slip into the side door at school to retrieve our book bags from our lockers. A handful of students are still walking around, heading to or finishing after-school activities. Poke and I live three blocks from school, two houses apart. We walk to and from school together most days. The walk home is silent. Poke has taken out his lucky dollar and rubs it the entire way home. All I do is keep picturing the rows of finger bones buried in the woods. I wave goodbye to Poke and watch him disappear into his house.

At dinner that night I find I don't have much of an appetite. I push the pile of spaghetti on my plate around with my fork, and it makes me think of the tangled roots of the uprooted tree.

"You feel all right, Drake?" my mother asks. "You're not eating."

"I'm fine. Just not hungry," I say.

I glance at my dad, who's staring at me.

"Something happen at school?" Dad asks. "Want to talk about it?"

"Really, I'm fine," I say. "I got a huge math test tomorrow I'm worried about. I should probably go study. May I be excused?"

My parents exchange a look before they both nod. They're not stupid and I know they can tell something is bothering me. Experience has taught me that they'll leave me alone for a while, but one of them, Dad most likely, will come up to my room to see if I want to talk it out. Part of me hopes so, too. I'm scared about what Poke and I found. Having had several hours to think about it, I know that whoever is buried in our town's woods shouldn't be there and someone should be told.

That thought stays in my head for another half hour until I can't take it anymore. I don't wait for Mom or Dad to come to my room. I walk downstairs to the family room where they are watching *Seinfeld* reruns.

"Can I talk to you guys?" I say.

Dad clicks off the TV.

I lay it out for them. How Connor told us about the intact wolf skeleton he and his friends found in the woods behind school; how he dared Poke and me to check it out; how we found where Connor told us to go; how we discovered the bones of a person's arm and hand. After I finish, my father takes out his cell phone and calls the police. Ten minutes later, I am retelling my story to a pair of officers. When I finish, they go out to their car but don't drive off. After maybe ten minutes, they knock on the door again. They want me and my dad to show them exactly where I found the bones. It's dark out at that point and I know it will be even darker in the woods. I'm not sure I want to find the spot at night.

The officers have powerful flashlights, and once we get to Cougar Rock it turns out to be fairly easy to navigate to the site of the fallen tree. I'm wearing a jacket, but standing in those dark woods I am colder than I've ever felt before. Once the police officers confirm that what I told them is true, they radio for backup and forensics. After help arrives, one of the police officers drives my dad and me back home.

Our discovery in the woods becomes the biggest news our town has known in a long time. For three weeks, the woods behind our school are taped off by the police as they search for other bodies, but they never find any others. News reports indicate that the body belonged to a middle-aged man, and that DNA testing is being done. But they say that, due to decomposition, identification might be impossible.

At school, Poke and I are celebrities, all the kids probing us for the gory details about what we found. Poke entertains our classmates with the story of how he found the body when he tripped on it and pushed his hand down right onto the arm bone. Neither of us has ever been too popular and I can tell that Poke enjoys the attention. I'd be lying if I didn't say it is kind of fun. Connor is pissed at us, however, angry that he didn't get all the credit since he was the one who found the first bones, which the cops say is only a dog and not a wolf.

But a month later, when a local gas station attendant is shot and killed in a botched robbery, the story of the body in the woods fades from everyone's attention. Another month goes by with no new information. Poke and I go back to being a couple of ignored nerds.

Then one day, I walk into my house after school to find both my mother and father waiting for me, the expressions on their faces serious. I can tell my mom has been crying. My mouth goes dry and my stomach tightens.

"Come sit down, Drake," Dad says. "We need to tell you something."

I unhook the strap of my backpack and lean the bag against the bottom step of the staircase leading upstairs to the bedrooms. I fight an urge to run up the steps. Instead, I walk into the living room and drop into the chair facing the sofa, where my parents are sitting side by side. I wait for one of them to speak first. It's Dad.

"Drake, we just spoke with Austin's mother."

Even my parents usually call my best friend "Poke," so I know whatever they're about to tell me is super serious. Less than five minutes ago I watched Poke head inside his own house, and I imagine he is likely sitting in his own living room, listening to his mother explain whatever it is I'm about to learn.

"Son, the police have identified the body you and Austin found. It turns out that the person was Austin's father. He'd been murdered. The animal your other friend found was their dog, Lucy."

In the next moment, I have the sensation of all the blood in my body sinking to my feet. I look at my dad for a long time, and then look at my mom, who has started crying again.

"When did they find out?" I ask.

"They confirmed it today," Mom says. "Some policemen were down at Mrs. Fitzgerald's house until about twenty minutes ago. She called us after they left."

I sit silently, looking at my sneakers. I can still see faint traces of dried mud from when I fell in the woods that day. My parents wait for me to speak.

"Poke's dad was murdered?" I ask, not knowing what else to say.

"He was shot," Dad says. "And so was Lucy."

I'm hot and cold at the same time and I'm desperate to

get out of the room. "Can I go upstairs? I've got a lot of homework."

"Sure thing, kiddo," Dad says. "Let me know if you need to talk."

I stand quickly, my legs a bit wobbly, and hurry out of the room. When I reach my bedroom, I shut the door and flop onto my bed. Lying there, all I can do is think about Poke. He has to know by now. I wonder how he's taking the news. Outside my bedroom's window the afternoon sky is hard blue, without a single cloud to distract my thoughts. I slide my cell phone from my pocket and tap Poke's number. I listen as it rings, closing my eyes to imagine Poke checking the screen two houses away, but after five rings it switches to voicemail. Poke always answers when I call. When the beep sounds for me to leave my message, I hang up. Poke knows I called and he'll call me back when he feels like talking. Besides, I'm a little relieved he didn't answer. I have no idea what to say to him.

In the morning, while I'm getting ready for school, Poke texts me to say he won't be walking with me. His mom wants him to stay home for a few days because of the news about his father.

Somehow, a lot of the kids at our school have already heard that Poke's dad was murdered and, since I'm Poke's best friend, many of them come to ask me if I have any information. Others seem anxious to tell me the rumors they've heard—that Mr. Fitzgerald was a drug dealer and got killed because of a bad deal with the Mexican cartel, or that he killed the dog and then committed suicide because of money problems he was hiding from his family. A girl named Brianna with severe acne, who sits in front of me in my social studies class, turns around to inform me she has it on good authority that Poke's dad was an ex-agent for the CIA and was targeted by Islamic terrorists. Brianna can't understand why they had to kill Lucy, too, however. It's only when she mentions the dog that she seems to get upset. All I can think of is how hard it will be for poor Poke to have to hear all this bullshit when he comes back to school.

But Poke never comes back to school. I speak with him on the phone most days and he tells me how his mom is different since she found out about the murder. She quit her job as a receptionist at a law firm and hired a real estate agent to sell their house. Within two weeks Mrs. Fitzgerald settles on an apartment to rent in Raleigh, three hours away. Then, one month to the day after I sat in the living room listening to my parents tell me the bones we'd discovered were my best friend's father and dog, Poke comes by my house to say goodbye. We go up to my bedroom, the place where we've hung out for years discussing anything and everything.

"I can't believe you're moving away," I say.

"Me either. It's messed up." We both nod and don't say anything for a minute. "I'm really worried about my mom."

"Yeah, she doesn't seem to be taking this well. I overheard my parents talking and they said she's having some kind of breakdown."

I realize immediately I shouldn't have said that and shoot a quick look at Poke but he seems not to have heard. He's sitting on the end of my bed picking at a loose thread on the knee of his jeans.

"Well, I just came over to say goodbye. I better get going," Poke says. "Mom wants to get an early start tomorrow."

I nod, unable to speak because of a sudden tightness in my chest. Poke stands and punches me on the shoulder before walking toward the bedroom door. He stops abruptly and turns back to face me.

"I almost forgot. There's something I want to give you." Poke reaches into the pocket of his jeans and removes his lucky silver dollar. "I want you to have this."

I stare at the polished coin sitting on his open palm. "I can't take that, Poke. It's your good luck charm."

"I think any luck in it for me was used up a long time ago," he says. "But maybe you can still find some."

He extends his arm and waits while I get off the bed and come over. I take the dollar reluctantly.

"Thanks, buddy," I say, then step closer and hug him. I feel my eyes starting to burn and fight hard not to cry in front of my best friend.

We separate and Poke hurries out of my room without saying anything more. I hear his quick, heavy footsteps as he runs down the stairs and I don't move until long after I hear the front door slam shut. I go sit on the edge of my bed and wonder if I'll ever see my best friend again. I rub my trembling thumb across the smooth surface of the dollar, faster and faster and faster, making a wish I know will never come true.

Best Laid Plans

1

After Stewart's father suffered a calamitous heart attack at the age of fifty-six, it fell upon Stewart to perform the preponderance of duties his dad had been responsible for, chiefly those involving maintenance at his parents' home. And not only at his parents' house, but also, and more often, at Stewart's grandmother's house. Dorothy (Stewart never knew her as anything else as she refused to be called grandma, nana, or anything other than her given name) was two months shy of her ninetieth birthday and stubbornly independent. She lived in a small brick ranch house in a modest neighborhood of Winston-Salem, the city where they all resided. Dorothy's house was where Stewart's father had spent his childhood. Despite more than two decades of pleading from Stewart's parents for his grandmother to move into their home, Dorothy refused to leave.

So late one Saturday in July, after a long, tedious, and sweaty day of yard work at his own home, then his father's, and lastly at Dorothy's house, Stewart sat exhausted at his grandmother's kitchen table while she fixed him supper. The two of them had a long conversation in which Stewart detailed the tribulations of trying to maintain three households, emphasizing how he was unable to spend as much time with his four-year-old daughter as he used to. Maybe it was the uttermost exhaustion Dorothy heard in her grandson's voice that night, or perhaps the mention of the effect on her great-granddaughter (who was named Dottie after her), that changed her heart, but Dorothy told Stewart that very evening that, if he was willing, she would sell her house and move in with his family.

Through a combination of Stewart's hard work and a good deal of luck, Dorothy's house sold within two months of her decision and she left the only home she'd known for over sixty years to move across town to her grandson's big, two-story house in one of the city's oldest historic neighborhoods. However, still as independent as ever, Dorothy refused to allow Stewart to convert his first-floor office into a bedroom for her, insisting she occupy the spare bedroom on the second floor. Early one morning of the first week after Dorothy moved in, she dressed to head downstairs to cook breakfast for Stewart before he left for work. She misjudged the second stair and tumbled down the long flight, her head crashing against the newel post, which caused rapid and significant hemorrhaging that killed her in less than three minutes.

2

Phillip was a great writer. Nearly everyone who read his work said so. And they meant it. While there was undoubtedly innate talent involved, Phillip worked hard for many years to hone his craft. His passion for words was evident in the high literary quality of the short fiction he wrote. He was much published, but almost exclusively in literary journals and magazines that few people outside the world of academe or the writing community had ever read. He won many awards and garnered praise from the editors of these journals, yet the general public did not know his name or his work. Phillip consoled himself with the belief that he wrote the stories he wanted to write, stories that were richly layered and carefully constructed with nuances and metaphors whose meaning went well beyond the surface plot. In this he succeeded. But after years of receiving critical reward but little in the way of financial compensation, Phillip started feeling resentful of all the hard work he poured into his writing. And despite the fact he had an understanding and supportive wife, who worked diligently without complaint to support their modest but comfortable lifestyle, Phillip's desire for commercial success grew slowly over a number of years until he made the decision to attempt to write a mainstream novel, hopeful it would achieve at least a moderate degree of commercial success.

Before long, Phillip had developed a plot for a clever crime thriller, spending the first few months outlining the story with plot twists and intrigue he felt certain the general public would love. But ever the serious writer, Phillip spent five years on this endeavor, going through draft after draft until he was satisfied he'd created an exciting and readable novel. On the day he finished the book, he made two digital copies on separate flash drives and placed them in a locked drawer in his desk. Exhilarated, Phillip arranged to take his wife that evening to Winston-Salem's most elegant and expensive restaurant to celebrate.

At dinner, Phillip ordered champagne and they ate a spectacular meal. He and his wife fantasized at length about all the things they would do if his book became a bestseller— buy a nicer house in a better neighborhood, travel to all the places they'd only talked about over the years, and, most importantly, spend more time together. As they left the restaurant to head home, Phillip and his wife were tipsy and giddy and the happiest they'd been in a long while. When the valet pulled their car to the curb in front of the restaurant, Phillip's wife slid into the passenger seat as Phillip reached into his left pocket for cash to tip the valet. His arm went suddenly numb and Phillip felt as though someone had dropped a massive weight on his chest. It was merely a second after Phillip realized he was having a heart attack that he collapsed unconscious onto the sidewalk. The maître d' was trained in CPR and attempted to keep Phillip alive until the paramedics arrived, but he was dead by the time they got him to the hospital.

Phillip's widow thought frequently about the novel sitting locked in her husband's desk, but she blamed the stress of writing it and his fear of failure for his death, so for a long time she wanted nothing to do with it. But several years later, as she was packing the house to move to a smaller, more affordable home in another town on the other side of the state, she held the memory sticks containing the final draft of Phillip's book, debating whether to throw them away. In the end, she decided to keep them. After settling in her new place she contacted a literary agent with the manuscript. The agent was impressed and agreed to shop it to publishers. It was picked up quickly by one of the nation's largest publishing houses, a rare thing for a first novel, and became the most talked about and popular book of the year. Phillip's widow eventually made millions of dollars from royalties, met another man, whom she fell in love with, and subsequently spent many years travelling with her new husband to most of the places she'd always planned to visit with Phillip.

3

At eighteen years of age, Kyra had already known her share of tragedy and misery. Her parents had died in a plane crash when she was nine, after which she was shuffled from family member to family member for more than a year before ending up in South Dakota with the family of an uncle she'd not met until she moved in. A popular girl in elementary school back in her hometown in Oregon, Kyra never fit in well at her new school in Pierre, mostly because her cousins, who also attended the school, resented having to share their things, and made fun of Kyra and taunted her whenever adults were not around. Kyra would cry herself to sleep most nights during the first year she lived with her uncle's family.

In high school, things had been no better for Kyra, again thanks to the ostracizing of her mean-spirited cousins. As a defense against this pariahdom, Kyra turned inward, spending the majority of her spare time alone reading, studying, and writing poetry. She never attended school events unless they were mandatory, or her uncle and aunt forced her. Her grades were superior and at graduation she was class valedictorian, a status that only enraged her popular cousins, whose grades were mediocre at best. At a graduation party thrown by Kyra's aunt and uncle at their house, Kyra's cousins and their friends grabbed her, pulled her out into the backyard, and forced most of a fifth of vodka down her throat until she gagged and vomited, inhaling so much of the liquor she needed to be rushed to the hospital for treatment of aspiration pneumonia.

So it was no surprise Kyra viewed going to college as an escape; it would be a new start to what she told herself was, at last, her real life. Her GPA ensured admittance to nearly any school she chose, and she received many academic scholarships. Kyra selected Wake Forest University in North Carolina, primarily in an attempt to get as far as possible from South Dakota and her cousins. But after nearly a decade of forced social awkwardness Kyra had difficulty making friends at her new college. Her freshman-year roommate, a townie who'd grown up in Winston-Salem, was rarely around on weekends and had few shared interests with Kyra. So, once again, she immersed herself in her studies. When the first year of classes ended in the spring, she found a summer job as a hostess at a local restaurant, the salary from which was just enough to allow her to rent a small efficiency apartment, which she kept after school started again in August.

But being all alone night after night in her tiny apartment only allowed Kyra to dwell on her profound loneliness. So late one Tuesday, her night off from the restaurant, after spending hours alone in her claustrophobic flat with nothing other than her own self-pitying thoughts, Kyra decided to walk the short distance from her apartment to Interstate-Business 40, at an exit that provided a high overpass so she could jump off in front of a vehicle speeding along the expressway and put an end, once and for all, to her despondency. The night was warm, but a light breeze raised goosebumps on Kyra's arms as she stood at the waist-high concrete wall, looking toward the oncoming traffic. Ever the deep thinker, she'd analyzed her plan on the walk over and reasoned she'd best wait for a semi-truck in order to ensure a successful suicide. It wasn't long before Kyra spied a truck approaching from no more than a half mile up the road. She climbed up on the wall and swung both legs over until she was in a sitting position, ready to push off at the right moment. While Kyra stared intently at the oncoming semi, she hadn't noticed that a car had pulled over near her. A young man Kyra's age, heading to a campus party, noticed the girl sitting on the bridge's wall and had stopped. Mere seconds before Kyra was about to jump he called to her, distracting her while the truck passed below.

The young man, assessing quickly what was happening, hurried over to Kyra, grabbed her arm, and insisted she come back onto the bridge. More embarrassed than angry,

Kyra complied. The young man, named Will, talked to her for ten minutes and convinced her to allow him to drive her home. Will and Kyra sat on her tiny sofa talking all night, the sad girl opening her heart for the first time to the stranger who'd saved her life. It was mid-morning when Will finally left Kyra's apartment, but not before arranging to have dinner with her that night. After six months of dating, the two fell in love and were married one year following graduation, on the fourth anniversary of Kyra's attempted suicide. They remained happily married for sixty-eight years, having three children, seven grandchildren, eighteen great-grandchildren, and four great-great-grandchildren, all of whom Kyra and Will got to meet before dying two weeks apart of natural causes at the age of ninety.

Swing

The house is too silent. Garland stands at the screen door staring across the dry, fallow front field. It's hot outside. Hot enough for old thirsts to tempt him. But there is no beer in the fridge now. None for nearly two years. *But, boy, this is a day made for beer*, Garland thinks. He lets his eyes drift closed and remembers the wonderfully cold bite in his throat after the first sip, so familiar back then. Garland swallows reflexively from the muscle memory earned after so many years, so many drinks.

A cooling breeze pushes across the porch, strong enough to cause the swing to begin swaying, drawing Garland's attention. The fond memory of cold beer suddenly sours and he fights not to vomit. He squeezes his eyes against the burning in his gullet, in his stomach. In his heart.

When he opens his eyes again, he's unable to keep from watching the chipped and peeling swing, hazed through the fine mesh of the screen, slowing and slowing but never settling. Behind him the house is still and silent. Too silent to keep out the sounds in Garland's head—the rattle of the swing's chains, the loud crack that followed, his wife's screams as he carried the baby into the house.

No One's Ghost but My Own

My wife calls out my name, startling me awake. I dig my knuckles into my eyeballs to rub out the burning and, truth be told, to delay the awkward conversation I know is about to ensue. As I open my eyes and look at her—toward her, I guess is more accurate—my eyes focus on the indistinct shape of the dresser behind her, blurred by the translucence of her body. She wants to buy a new dress, she tells me, and needs me to order it for her online. I remind her—for the umpteenth time—dead women don't need dresses, new or otherwise.

It's not like Franci doesn't know she's dead. She has been gone for just over a year now, although her visits began only in the past month. I was terrified at first. I'd jolt awake to see her suspended a foot off the floor and I'd scream, lying awake with the lights on the rest of the night as she kept trying to get me to acknowledge her, until she got tired or frustrated enough by my pretending she wasn't there to dissolve away to nothing. Those first half dozen times I convinced myself I was hallucinating, that these visions of my dead wife were merely manifestations of deep-seated, unresolvable marital conflicts my mind and heart struggled to settle while I slept. But after so many visits I've come to accept it really is her ghost. And now, every night, she comes begging me to open up my laptop and order her a dress.

"And why do you need a new dress?" I ask yet again, my voice betraying sleep-deprived irritation at this exasperating routine we've developed.

Franci looks down, embarrassed.

Only now does it occur to me that this must be weird for her, too. Her form starts to shimmer and flicker, reminding me of the crew from the *Star Trek* TV shows when they were transporting down to a planet. I can barely make out that Franci is picking at a spot on an invisible fingernail.

"Listen," I say, "I'm not saying I won't buy you the dress; it just seems like something you wouldn't really need, you know, now."

Franci looks up then, still hovering next to the bed—the same bed she and I made love on countless times and in which we conceived our son, Danny—and the odd sparkling stops.

"Don't you think that dead girls like to look pretty, too?" she asks.

She glides away then, passing straight through the bedroom wall. I stare at the spot, waiting for her to reemerge, but she doesn't. I glance at my clock and see it is three hours before the alarm will go off. Since it's obvious I won't be able to go back to sleep, I slide out of bed, figuring I'll go down to the kitchen and make some coffee.

When I'm halfway down the stairs, I notice Franci floating in the living room, her back to me. She appears to be staring at the photographs lined along the mantel above the fireplace.

I walk over and stand next to my wife and look at the pictures with her. In the center is one of the three of us taken at Danny's college graduation less than two years ago, not long before Franci's diagnosis. The picture directly in front of me, the oldest of the photographs, is from our wedding day. The two of us look almost unrecognizable, so young and vital. Franci is dazzling in her white gown, grinning that smile that never failed, in thirty years, to make me feel like the luckiest man alive. I'm standing a little behind her, awkward in my tuxedo, squinting at the camera with a slightly dazed expression, a mix of naiveté and cockiness, thinking I was ready to take on all that life would toss at us.

"I wish I looked like that again," Franci says, watching me as I study the photo.

"You always will," I say. "You never stopped looking that pretty. Not once. I just didn't tell you that enough."

Franci reaches out to pick up the photo from Danny's graduation but her hand wafts right through it. I lift it up for her and hold it so we both can see. A question bursts into my mind just then and I wonder why it hadn't occurred to me sooner.

"Have you visited Danny, too?"

She looks at me, her expression neutral, unreadable. "Not yet, honey. I will when I think he's ready. For now, I'm no one's ghost but your own."

Her answer feels like a soft punch to my heart. I recall instantly the time I asked Franci out on our first date. We'd started graduate school together. I noticed her right away at orientation, but I convinced myself she was too beautiful to consider dating someone like me. Yet I somehow screwed up the nerve to ask anyway and, to my surprise, she said yes. Even after three or four dates, I was still certain I was only someone for her to hang out with until Mr. Right came along. I vividly recall lying to her one night as we sat on the lumpy couch in my tiny apartment, telling her I'd be okay if she wanted to date other guys. Franci punched me on the shoulder —not hard—and pulled my face close to hers, saying, "I am no one's girl but your own." I found her odd way of phrasing her words unique and charming, and I never forgot it.

Then this memory is followed rapidly by others: Franci burning three consecutive batches of cookies she was baking for Danny's kindergarten class, setting off the smoke alarms in two rooms; Franci crying for two days when our pet guinea pig died; Franci getting drunk one night and insisting on putting polish on my toenails and not taking no for an answer. I remember a string of silly things about her I'd thought I'd forgotten—wearing my underwear on her head, the awful Elvis impersonation she did every time she had a couple drinks, and especially her obsession with buying new dresses.

"I'll see you tomorrow," Franci says, pulling me out of my reverie. She sails up through the living room ceiling and disappears.

"Good night, darling," I say to the empty room, and I feel tears on my face.

I'm tired now, so I skip the coffee and plod back upstairs to try and sleep for an hour or so before I have to get up for work. I stop in Danny's old bedroom, which I've converted to a home office, and collect my laptop to leave on my bedside table for Franci's next visit.

Lying in bed, drowsy, my thoughts fixate on Franci and dresses. I find myself hoping she'll pick a green one, my favorite color on her. But if she decides on white, that'll be just fine. And I wonder, will she even be able to wear it if I order it? Then a disturbing thought occurs to me: will Franci leave me alone again once she's gotten from me what she's asking for? And I realize it's this that haunts me most of all.

Custody Battle

The banging in my head takes on the same beat as the rapping on my door. I squeeze my eyes tight, hoping the knocking is merely the tail end of a hangover-driven dream.

"Open up, Joe! I don't have time for this."

When I crack open the door, bright sunlight burns my throbbing eyeballs. My ex-wife, Jeanette, is standing on the porch looking at her watch. Her blonde hair is several shades lighter than I remember and frames her face in elegant waves. She's all made up and I can smell a hint of some delightful perfume I don't recognize. She looks amazing.

"Christ, Joe," Jeanette says, "Were you still sleeping? It's after noon."

"It's my day off."

"So I smell," she says.

That's when I notice our fifteen-year-old son, Kenny, behind her. He lives full-time with his mother, but Jeanette had called me earlier in the week and asked if Kenny could spend one night with me because she had some work-related thing that's supposed to run late.

"Shit, I forgot. I'm sorry, Kenny." Over Jeanette's shoulder I see Kenny nod.

"Really?" Jeanette says. "I asked you just two days ago about this and already it's slipped your mind?"

My stomach roils, filling my throat with a sharp, rancid burn.

"Easy, Jeanie. It's all good." I look at my son and grin. "When do you need him home?"

"No later than six tomorrow," Jeanette says. "He's got a big chemistry final on Monday and needs to study, which I doubt he'll do here." She glances over her shoulder at the patchy scrub grass in front of my shithole of a rental house. "Although out here in the boonies I'm not sure what else he *could* do. I've never understood why you choose to live out in the middle of nowhere, Joe."

I pull the door fully open so Kenny can come inside. I watch his mother give him a quick kiss on the cheek before he steps around her.

"You guys have fun, Mom," Kenny says. "See you tomorrow."

I lift my eyebrows at Jeanette, who frowns at Kenny. She flips me the bird and hurries back to her car. I watch her check her hair and makeup in the car's rearview mirror before backing out of the driveway.

When I shut the door and turn around, Kenny is grinning. He is tall, a good inch taller than I am, and good-looking, on the cusp of becoming handsome, with a thick mop of dark, curly hair (my contribution) with Jeanette's bright, intelligent green eyes.

"She's got a date with a new boyfriend," he says. "Or should I say 'sleepover'?"

"That right?"

"Yeah. She didn't want me to say anything to you, but I figured you didn't really care," he says, and gives me another grin.

"Don't worry. I don't," I say. But that's a lie and I again experience regrets I've felt often in the five years since I lost Jeanette. Other than Kenny, she was easily the best thing I'd ever had, and I fucked it up. My temples begin to throb again.

"Sorry the place is such a mess, kiddo. I'd have straightened up if I'd remembered."

"No worries, Dad." He unslings his backpack and tosses it on the end of the couch.

"You hungry, or want something to drink? I haven't got much, but I'm sure I can find something."

"How about a beer?" Kenny asks.

I gaze at him to see if he's joking. I don't think he is, and in that moment I realize how much my son looks like me. And how badly I stink of booze.

"I don't think that'd be wise."

We both nod.

Kenny unzips his bag and slides out his laptop. "Figured it didn't hurt to ask. Got any soda?"

"There should be some ginger ale. Help yourself." Kenny starts for the kitchen. "Hey, son, do you mind if I grab another hour or so of shuteye? I'm feeling a bit rocky. We'll figure out something to do later, when I'm a tad steadier."

"Sure thing," he says. "You still got WiFi?"

I nod and ignore the unspoken implication about my financial situation. Kenny heads into the kitchen.

My bedroom is bright despite the shades being drawn. A band of sunlight sneaking in at the edge of the window cuts across the bottom of my bed. I figure at this point I won't be able to sleep long, if at all, but I lie down just to ease the pounding at my temples.

Two hours later, Kenny shakes me awake. The light in the room has dimmed and the line of light has crawled halfway up the wall opposite my bed.

"Dad, wake up. There's someone here." I smell beer on Kenny's breath.

"Who is it?"

"He wouldn't say. Just said I'd better get you fast." Kenny looks quickly over his shoulder toward the bedroom door. I can see he's scared.

My head doesn't hurt as bad as before, but sitting up takes considerable effort.

"Did he say what he wanted?"

Kenny shakes his head. I snatch a pair of crumpled jeans that are draped over the end board and slip them on. "What does he look like?"

"Big and bald," he says. "And scary."

"Does he have a thick scar crossing over the bridge of his nose?"

"Yeah. Who is it, Dad?"

"His name is Holt. I need you to stay in here while I talk to him. Do you understand me, Kenny?"

"Sure."

In the living room, Holt is sitting on the couch looking at the screen on Kenny's computer. When he sees me, he stands up and moves one hand around his back and leaves it there. I've no doubt he's got a gun. Holt's not the type to take chances.

"We need our money, Joe," Holt says.

Holt is the collector for the bookie I've used for the past year. He'd be scary-looking even if he didn't have that damned scar across his wide, bulldog face. At six-foot-two he and I may be the same height but he outweighs me by at least a hundred pounds.

"I thought I had until next week."

Holt grins. "Well, you thought wrong. Now give me what you owe and then you can go back to playing with your kid."

"Listen, Holt, I got most of it. Just give me until Monday and I'll have it all." I glance down the hall toward the bedroom.

"My son's here. I don't want him to have to see any more of his old man being a loser."

"That's your problem. Mine is, if I don't go back with all of what you owe, then *I'm* the one in trouble. I don't plan on being in trouble because of a shitbag like you." He reaches up and slides a cell phone from his shirt pocket. "You want, I can call Jenkins and ask him how he wants me to handle this?"

Holt and I are equally aware of what the answer to that would be.

"There's no need for that, Holt," I say. "I'm sure we. . ."

Just then Holt's gaze shifts to the right and he whips out the handgun that was in his waistband and points it down the hall. I turn to see Kenny standing there with his eyes wide, his arms extended with his palms out.

"What the hell's going on, Dad?"

I turn to Holt. "Put the fucking gun away. He's got nothing to do with this."

Holt's eyes shifts from Kenny to me, then back. "It's simple, Joe. Give me the money and no one gets hurt." He drops his phone back into his pocket and grips the gun in both hands.

The pulsing in my head amps up and I can feel my heart pounding like I've just run a marathon.

"Come on, Holt, let's talk about this calmly," I say.

Holt then cocks the hammer on the gun and edges the barrel up so it's aimed at Kenny's head. I rush forward and kick my leg up fast, knocking the gun with the sole of my bare foot. It flies out of Holt's grip. The pistol arcs away, bouncing off the wall to land on the floor a foot or so from Kenny, who darts to it and picks it up. Kenny aims the gun at Holt. I can see my son's hand is shaking like crazy.

"Get out of this house, asshole!" Kenny shouts, his eyes never wavering from the big goon in my living room.

Holt starts walking slowly toward Kenny. "You'll want to give that gun to me now, boy. We don't want anyone getting hurt."

"Stop where you are," Kenny says. Holt keeps advancing. I hurry over and grab Holt's arm to pull him back. It feels like I'm holding a steel pipe. He swings the fist of his other hand but I manage to duck underneath the punch, letting go of my grip on his arm. Holt swivels and grabs my neck in a headlock. I flail weak punches at his midsection, which makes him squeeze tighter on my neck. I struggle to get air. Tiny, bright dots fill my vision as I start to faint. My legs buckle. Then I hear a shot and the pressure on my neck is gone. I fall onto my side and see Holt on the floor next to me, moaning and pressing both hands over the inside of his thigh. Blood oozes between his fingers and runs down his leg onto the faded green carpet.

"You shot me, you little prick!" Holt says. He's glaring at Kenny, who stands frozen with his arm extended, the gun still pointing straight ahead.

I manage to scramble up and take the gun away from him. He is pale and trembling all over.

"I think we'd better get out of here," I say.

Holt tries to push himself up. "You and your kid just made a big fuckin' mistake, Joe. I hope you know that."

Holt gets onto his good knee and attempts to stand. I walk over and drive my foot directly onto the bleeding hole in his other leg. While Holt screams, I tell my son to wait outside while I grab my car keys and wallet from my bedroom. Kenny hurries out of the house and I run over and snatch Holt's cell phone from his shirt pocket before running down the hall. I hear Holt's groaning, and when I return his leg is gushing blood. He's panting, worried, as he looks to me with pleading eyes.

"This is bad, Joe," Holt says. "At least. . .dial 911 before you leave. I need an ambulance. I could bleed to death."

I glance at Holt's leg and see he's likely correct. Underneath his leg, spreading fast, is a huge puddle of blood. More blood than I've ever seen. The bullet must have hit an artery.

Kenny pokes his head through the front door. "Come on, Dad. We gotta go. Just leave him. That asshole was going to kill *me*, remember?"

I stand there in my living room, frozen, unsure what to do. Finally I hurry toward the door. Before shutting it, I take one last look at Holt.

Once outside, I lock the dead bolt. I figure if Holt ever manages to scramble up, he'll have at least a small obstacle to getting the door open, which in his weakened state might be difficult. When I turn away from the house, Kenny is already standing next to my beat-up Malibu, his hand gripping the door handle. I hurry over and unlock the car. When we get in, I lean across Kenny to open the glove box and toss Holt's gun inside.

"We'll get rid of that as soon as we get a chance," I say. Kenny nods. "Where will we go?"

"I have no idea. We'll have to figure that out on the road." I jab the key into the ignition.

Holt had parked his Expedition right behind my Chevy, nearly touching bumpers, no doubt so I couldn't escape before he got my money. I have to pull up and back several times until I get enough of an angle to drive across the lawn toward the dirt road in front of the house. With each change of direction I glance at my front door, expecting it to fly open and Holt to limp out. I lower the car's windows. I can hear Holt yelling for help. I guide the car onto the road and accelerate, a cloud of dust and pebbles kicking up behind us.

I head west on I-40 and we drive for a good half hour without speaking. I keep glancing over at Kenny, who is silently staring out the passenger window at the rushing landscape.

"Thank you for saving my life, son," I say at last. When he turns to look at me I can see his eyes are moist and red. "I know you didn't have any other choice."

"Am I gonna go to jail?" His lower lip is trembling.

"No. That's not going to happen. I shot him. You got that? And it was self-defense. Nothing is going to happen to you." The words sound hollow. Fact is I have no idea how this is going to play out. The thought does occur to me I should just call the cops and lay it out for them, but I think about Jenkins' reaction. And Jeanette's.

Up ahead I glimpse a billboard advertising a motel near Lake Lure called The Amity Inn. The ad shows a row of cabins in front of red and yellow and green mountains lit up by an idealized sunset. The lake is another forty-five minutes away. I'd taken Kenny fishing up there once when he was four or five, back before I mistakenly thought I was a good enough poker player to give Jeanette and Kenny the great lives I felt I wasn't giving them. The lake is far enough away to give me time to think. I decide we'll hole up there and sort things out.

"Hey, kiddo. Remember when we went fishing at Lake Lure? You were pretty small."

Kenny doesn't answer, just stares out the window and bites his lip.

"I'm gonna head up there so we can figure out our next step, okay? It'll be good to be in the mountains again. Maybe we can hike up to Chimney Rock."

When I look at Kenny he is nodding but no longer smiling.

"Too bad we didn't come up with this idea before that guy Holt showed up," he says, then turns and leans his head against the window.

Suddenly, Holt's cell phone, which I'd tossed on the seat between us, begins to buzz. The screen IDs the caller only as "J."

"Should we toss the phone out the window?" Kenny asks.

I consider that, but then think better of it. Cell phones can be traced with GPS. A sign on my right indicates two miles to our exit. The phone stops buzzing.

"Text him back," I say.

Kenny picks up the phone.

"Jenkins is the guy who sent Holt to my place," I say. "He's probably wondering what's taking him so long. Text him that everything's cool and it won't be much longer."

As I slow the Malibu to take the exit for 221, Kenny slides his finger over the phone's screen. "He's got it password protected."

"Shit."

"Hang on, Dad."

Kenny bites his lower lip and stares down at the phone. He tries entering a code, then another with no luck. On the third try, he smiles and holds up the phone triumphantly. "H-O-L-T. Some people are so stupid."

"Okay, send Jenkins the text."

Kenny types out the message. "Do you think he'll buy it?" he asks.

"I don't—" There's a loud ding as Jenkins' reply text comes right back. "What's he say?"

Kenny holds out the screen for me to see. "Read it to me. I'm driving," I say.

"It says, 'OK. Hurry.'" Kenny types something on the screen. "I told him, 'Yes, Sir.'"

I wonder for a moment if Holt is likely to ever call Jenkins "Sir." I press on the accelerator and push the Chevy up to sixty.

There are only a couple cars in The Amity Inn's lot when we pull in. The high season is at least a month away so we're able to rent a cabin easily. After I get checked in I pull the car in front of our cabin. I retrieve Holt's gun from the glove compartment and hide it under my shirt before climbing out of the car.

The air is cooler up here and directly across from the motel the Blue Ridge Mountains edge the sky in brilliant green. The air holds a lush, woodsy scent that is so pleasant I forget for a moment the reason we've come here.

Once inside, I hook the door chain and double-check the lock. I pull the curtains tight. Kenny turns on the lamp sitting on the small table between the room's two beds and then sits on the edge of one, looking at me.

"What do we do now?" he asks.

I go and sit across from him. "For now, we rest a bit. Why don't you watch TV?"

"I don't really feel like it, Dad. I'm pretty scared."

"I know, Kenny. I'm sorry I got you involved in this." I start to say more but don't really know what to say.

I lie back on the bed. I try to focus on what I need to do next but all I can manage to think about is how unlikely it is now that I will get to spend *any* time with Kenny from here on. On the wall across from me, above the television, is a cheesy watercolor of Lake Lure. Staring at it, I can see Kenny and me standing on the lake's soggy shoreline, and I'm helping him fit a nightcrawler onto his hook. He's grimacing as it wriggles wildly, and I assure him it's not in pain. Kenny nods and, after counting down from three, we toss our lines together into the lake. I remember thinking he's not likely to catch much with that toy rod, but soon enough he gets a strike. I help him reel it in and after we unhook a small crappie and release it, he starts jumping up and down, telling me to hurry and put more bait on his hook, all the time grinning like crazy.

If there's any way to find that connection again, I'd love to find it.

I stand up and empty my pockets. In one are my wallet and keys, which I place on the nightstand. In the other are two cell phones—Holt's and mine. I put my own on the bed and look for a moment at Holt's. I look around the room for something heavy, then remember the gun under my shirt. I take it out and empty the bullets onto the gold quilted bedspread. I walk over to a small desk opposite the bed, lay Holt's phone down and use the gun's butt as a hammer to smash it. I hit it once. A spider web crack spreads across the glass screen.

"Dad, why don't you just take out the SIM card and destroy that?" Kenny says.

"Take out what?"

Kenny comes over and picks up Holt's phone. "I need a paper clip, or something I can poke in a tiny hole with."

We scavenge through all the drawers. In one of the dresser drawers I find an abandoned safety pin. I hold it up and Kenny nods. I watch him insert the pin into a hole on the side of Holt's cell and a small door pops out. He slides it all the way out and lifts free a bitty black rectangle with gold stripes on one end. He holds it up for me to see.

"*This* is a SIM card. It's what identifies this particular phone and allows access to it from his service provider. We destroy this, no one can know where this phone is."

Kenny walks into the bathroom and I hear the toilet flush. He comes back and sits back in the same spot on the bed as before. I sit next to him and put my arm around his shoulders. He's trembling.

In my mind I try to frame all the things I want—I *need*—to say to my son. Nothing seems right.

"Kenny, I'm going to do my best to get us out of this mess. But at the very least, I'll make sure you're not involved in it any more. I promise."

He looks at me without saying anything and then nods. At that moment he looks no different than that little kid with the Ninja Turtles fishing rod.

"Listen, son," I say. "What happened today is something that should never have gone down. Today has shown me that I've allowed myself to sink to a level so low I wasn't even aware I was there. But when it was just me rolling around in the shit, well. . .I guess I deserved that. But now I've let that shit get on you. And I can't forgive myself for that."

"But if I hadn't been there you might've gotten hurt. Or worse."

The earnestness of his words hits me harder than any punch from Holt ever could. I stand up. "Come on, son. I'm taking you back to your mother's house."

"No, Dad. It's not safe back home."

"It'll be fine, Kenny. You have my word." I put my hand on his shoulder and squeeze. "C'mon, let's get out of here."

Kenny doesn't protest. We get back in the car. I don't bother checking out, just drive back toward the highway.

By the time we get back to Mocksville, the sky has darkened with only a hint of orange-pink at the horizon. As we pass the exit for my place, I subconsciously inch up my speed. Two exits later, I get off the Interstate and navigate through the town center, and when I turn onto Jeanette's street, Kenny puts his hand on my arm.

"What are you going to do, Dad?"

I park at the curb in front of my ex-wife's brick ranch. I turn off the engine, the click-click-click as it cools matching my own heartbeat. I scoot sideways to face Kenny. Past him, through the window, I see the drapes in the front window push aside and Jeanette look to see who's pulled up.

"I'm going to do my best to fix this. But you don't have to worry about it anymore."

"I want to help. This is my problem, too."

Behind Kenny I can see Jeanette in her robe, arms folded tight across her breasts, striding down the driveway. On her face is an expression that's equal parts anger and confusion.

"You *can* help. Don't tell your mother anything about Holt. Give her some story she'll believe. I'll take care of the rest."

Kenny pulls the door handle and starts to get out. He stops and leans back in and hugs me tight. "I love you, Dad."

"I love you, too. I'll be in touch soon. But remember— no matter what happens, you have to keep quiet about what went down today."

He nods, and then gets out. Kenny holds his hand up to stop his mother. He slams the car door and I watch him talking to his mother, who bends down to give me a dirty look. Kenny puts one arm behind his back and signals with a wave for me to drive away. I do.

When I pull up to my own house, my car's headlights reflect off the shiny black finish of Holt's Expedition. I lower my window and look at the front door, which is intact and unopened, and that tells me pretty much all I need to know. Still, just to be safe, I grab Holt's gun from the glove box and shut off the engine before walking cautiously to the door. When I turn the knob, I find the door still locked. I point the gun at the door and slide out my keys to unlock it. I ease the door open but only get a few inches before it bumps against an obstruction. Something big. Through the crack I spot Holt's outstretched arm. The skin of his forearm is gray, making the colors of the tattoo on it (crossed, bloody daggers) vivid and brilliant. I can just make out his wrist and hand, coated in drying blood.

I tug the door shut and leave it unlocked. I plop down on the small cement step and pull out my phone. When the 911 operator answers I tell her I need the police and an ambulance. She presses me for details and I tell her that I was home alone when someone knocked on my door. When I answered it, a man pushed his way into my house to rob me and we struggled. I managed to get his gun away and I shot him. I'm pretty sure he's dead, I tell her. The operator tells me to stay on the line until the police arrive, but I press the END button and power off the phone.

While I wait, I work on my story, repeating it over and over in my head so it'll come out naturally when I tell it to the cops. I'm doubtful they'll buy that I hid in my tool shed for so many hours until I was certain it was safe to come out, but it's all I can come up with. They'll simply wonder why I didn't just call from inside the shed or drive away, and forensics being what they are these days they're sure to know I drove my car across the lawn today. The bullshit I'll spin has more holes than a block of Swiss cheese, but I don't care. All I'm concerned about is that I can convince them I was home alone when Holt was shot.

I pat the pockets of my jeans and find my pack of cigarettes. I shake one out and light it, the first deep drag calming me a bit. I blow the smoke out slowly. When I go to drop the pack in my shirt pocket I notice there's something in there. It's the key card from The Amity Inn, with a photograph of Lake Lure on the front. It's gotten dark but there's still enough light to make out the picture. As I study it I pretend I can see a tiny version of Kenny standing at the lake's edge holding a tiny green fishing rod, and I'm unable to keep from grinning.

Blue and red lights appear down the road as the first of the cop cars arrive. I watch a sheriff's deputy get out and walk toward me, his hand on the butt of his gun. I take a final glance at the room card, slide it back in my pocket, and wait.

Fire and Ice

In a period of one month during my sophomore year of high school, I lost both my left eye and the heart of Carla Jean Buckner. I suppose enough time will pass that I'll consider the loss of my eye the more devastating event, but I'm not so sure.

All this occurred during January, the sluggish month when students are trying to shake off the torpor of the holidays. Amplifying this listlessness is the fact that I live in North Carolina, a place which, because it's perpetually poised on that climatic border of cold and warm air, is often subjected to ice storms. We'll have weeks at a time when everything—streets, houses, trees—is glazed in a beautiful coating of dazzling, but treacherous, ice. And while northern schools cancel classes for snow days, it's common for us Tarheels to shut down for "ice days." And it was on one such day of freedom from the tyranny of Reynolds High School that my best friend Stevie and I were horsing around outdoors, sliding down steep streets on nothing more than the soles of our boots (or our asses when our feet inevitably slid out from under us). Just as we got to the bottom of one such hill, we happened to notice a row of astonishingly massive icicles, like crystal stalactites, suspended from the eave of a nearby warehouse.

There must be something in the DNA of teenage boys that draws them to do things ordinary, sane humans would never do. Because without so much as one word of discussion, Stevie and I beelined to the vacant building and began jumping up to snap off these colossal chunks of ice. After we'd each managed to detach one, we stood amazed at the size of them and extended them out before us like knights' lances. So we did the natural thing for guys our age and began swinging them toward each other, hoping to demolish the other's icicle first. In one rapid arc I swung mine, sending it to a shattering collision with Stevie's, which in a cruel twist of the laws of physics, propelled the large pointed end of my own icicle straight back toward my face, where it lodged deep into the socket of my left eye, a mere half inch, I'd learn later, from piercing my brain.

The seriousness of what had just happened came not so much from the pain in my head, but from the sudden, shocked look on Stevie's face just before he doubled over and vomited. When his stomach was empty, he fumbled in his coat pocket to retrieve his cell phone to call 911, the whole time muttering *ohmygodohmygodohmygod*, his entire body shaking like he'd just been tasered. For my part, I knew I was in trouble, but I could only sit against the cold warehouse brick wondering why my left eye, or what used to be my left eye, felt so hot when it was packed with ice.

At the time of my blinding injury, Carla Jean and I had been dating for nearly six months. She was a junior at Reagan High School, across town from Reynolds. We'd met in July, when we both got summer jobs at the same Whole Foods. I noticed her on my first day. I was rolling a train of shopping carts toward the front of the store when

I caught sight of her assisting in the floral department. All I could see was her face, poised amid the roses and daisies and snapdragons as if it were just another bloom, and I couldn't take my eyes off her. She had dark blond hair tied back in a ponytail with a teal-colored ribbon, and a short row of bangs high up on her forehead. Her skin was lightly tanned and smooth with a sprinkling of freckles across her nose. Her lips glistened with pink gloss. When a customer tapped my shoulder, I jumped. She asked me if I was all right. I nodded and looked over to see if Carla Jean had noticed. The woman followed my gaze and smiled. She could see I was in love.

After that, I found ways to pass Carla Jean's station as often as I could. And when, one day, we found ourselves outside the store on our breaks, the sun hot and bright, I was amazed at how much prettier she was than I'd already thought. While we chatted mindlessly about our jobs and the brutal summer heat, I struggled to find a way to ask her on a date. Then, at a lull, she simply said, "We should go out sometime."

In all honesty, I'd never really had a girlfriend before I met Carla Jean. Sure, there were girls I'd hung out with at school, at football games, even girls I went to the movies with, but usually with Stevie or a group of our buddies. Certainly none I would claim to be in a real relationship with. So that summer following my freshman year of high school was a transformative one. Carla Jean and I spent all our free time together, often doing nothing more than hanging out at her parents' house watching TV or movies. We'd sit on one end of a long sofa and hold hands and she'd press her shoulder against mine so that I could smell her body wash, an intoxicating, flowery scent that at first I mistakenly thought was just the fragrance from the bouquets she'd worked on at Whole Foods still clinging to her clothes and skin. Hours passed during which I could not tell you what shows were on the television. I sat rigid, transfixed as Carla Jean did all the talking, regaling me with tales of her favorite musicians or the house at Wrightsville Beach that her family rented each summer or the brainy girl in her English class who she disliked. I took in every single word, watching her exquisite lips form each syllable, knowing somehow that she wanted me to lean over and kiss them, but struggling to find the nerve. And when at last I did, my whole body became suffused with a warmth yet to be exceeded by any other experience or sensation.

Once school restarted in the fall, I called Carla Jean every day. Unlike me, however, she was involved in activities and clubs—she was a cheerleader, of course—and I rarely got to see her except on weekends. But this dramatic drop in time together seemed to only strengthen our feelings for each other.

Until, that is, I gouged my eye out.

When I woke one morning with a bandage the size of a softball covering the place where my left eye used to be, Carla Jean was sitting next to my bed, holding my hand. I learned later I had been at Baptist Hospital for over two days while the doctors did surgery to clean out the mess I'd made of my face and to fix a blood vessel that stubbornly refused to stop hemorrhaging after the icicle melted enough to drop out of the socket. I smiled at the sight of Carla Jean. The vision of her face was almost better than the morphine, which I gauged from the fogginess in my brain, was assuredly dripping into my veins.

"Hi," she said. "You're an idiot." But she didn't say it mean and I could see she'd been crying. Then she winked and added, "And you actually look kind of sexy like this. Almost like a badass pirate. Maybe we should get you one of those buccaneer hats and an eye patch."

My mom and dad were standing at the end of the bed and they came over to hug me. That's when I learned how lucky I was to not be dead or brain damaged. They all stayed for about an hour before I started to doze off and the nurse shooed them out so I could rest. Carla Jean kissed me quickly on the lips and whispered, "I'll come see you again tomorrow." As I gave in to the opiate haze that was enveloping me, Carla Jean's beautiful, freckled face was all I saw.

But the next day Carla Jean didn't come by. Or the day after that. I got several text messages saying she was sorry but some big class projects were due, plus she'd already missed one cheerleading practice after she'd heard I was hurt and if she missed any more it might kill her chance at becoming squad captain. On the day of my discharge from the hospital, barely listening to the final instructions from the nurse, I stared at the door to my room, willing Carla Jean to walk through it and surprise me. She didn't.

And just like that, she stopped answering my texts and phone calls. We saw each other only once more, when she returned a few DVDs of mine. It was an awkward meeting. I opened the front door, surprised and more than a little excited to see her standing there. She wouldn't look me in the eye (that expression having a more literal meaning for me at that point), yet she seemed unable to keep from taking furtive glances at the slightly puckered medical patch covering the site of my injury. I tried to take her hand and lead her into the house but she just held onto the videos and leaned away. I desperately wanted to hold and kiss her so she could see that I was still the same idiot she'd loved before my accident.

"I'm sorry," she said.

"Sorry for what?"

She stared down at the cover of *Dumb and Dumber*. "It's hard to put into words."

I waited for her to say more, but she didn't. "Can you try?" I asked.

She bit her lower lip. "I don't know. Things are just. . . different now."

"'Things' aren't different, Carla Jean. *I'm* different. But I only lost my eye, not my heart."

"Don't you think I keep telling myself that? I guess I just need time to figure out how I feel."

Carla Jean thrust the DVDs at me and hurried away. I watched from the front door as she got into her car. She sat there for a couple minutes with her head down and I couldn't tell if she was crying. I held my breath, thinking she might change her mind and get out of the car and come back to tell me she was wrong and we could work things out. But then I saw her lift her head—and her cell phone—and I realized she was simply texting someone. As she backed out of the driveway she was talking on the phone and laughing.

When I returned to school, I'd become kind of a celebrity. The *Winston-Salem Journal* had published a story about me that was on the front page of the Sunday Local section. I still thought about Carla Jean, of course. In hindsight, I realize that I'd fooled myself when I thought someone like me could keep a beautiful girl like her. Heck, that she even gave me the time of day for six months strikes me as no small miracle. And now that enough time has passed, I sort of understand her side of things. We were in high school, after all. Carla Jean was one of the most popular girls at her school and, let's be honest, I was anything but popular at my own school. That is, until I lost my eye.

And the ironic thing is, until my eye socket healed enough for the prosthetic implant, my doctor had me wearing a black eye patch that Allie, a cute girl in my English class, said made me look really tough.

"You mean, sorta like a badass pirate?" I asked her.

She nodded and gave me a smile that made me realize everything would be just fine.

Snapped

After the phone call with my lawyer, I decide to take a walk around the neighborhood hoping to dispel some of the bitterness I'm feeling. My lawyer explained that my case is pretty much shit and that my wife is going to get my fishing boat. No matter how many times I tell him I'm suspicious Lorraine is sleeping with the guidance counselor at our kids' school, he counters that suspicion isn't proof, but phone records and eyewitnesses are. Which are the very things my wife has against me.

I love that boat. I remember struggling with whether we could afford it and Lorraine telling me, if it would make me happy, to just buy it. So I did. And the first time we took it out we made love in the cabin, the air heavy with the smell of salt and fish and sweat, our bodies rocking alternately with and against the bobbing of the waves. Now she wants to take it away from me.

I grab my jacket and slam the door on the way out of the house. When I turn the corner to head up the big hill on Clover Street, I spot a guy all the way at the top walking his dog, heading in my direction. The dog is tethered to one of those retractable leashes and I watch her—a small brown thing that looks like a tiny version of Lassie—zip away from the man to chase a squirrel, jerking to a stop when her owner presses the button to lock the cord. The dog trots back while the man reels in the leash. I'm in no mood for idle conversation, so as they get near I consider crossing the street. Before I can, the pup sees me, races up, and jumps up onto my legs, begging to be petted, her tail wagging so fast it's a blur. She's wearing a pink rhinestone collar whose tiny glass stones sparkle as they catch the sun.

"Sorry," the man says, catching up to his dog.

"No worries, I like dogs," I say. "My wife's allergic so I couldn't have one. Anyway, have a nice day."

I stand up from rubbing the dog's head and move past them quickly, continuing up the steep sidewalk. I go no more than ten steps when I hear a shout, the squeal of car tires, and a soft thud. I turn to see the man holding up the leash, the torn cord dangling from his hands, its frayed end still swinging. Glancing at the street, an old woman is sitting in her car with her hands covering her face. On the street in front of the vehicle the dog lies motionless, blood oozing from her nose and mouth.

"It snapped," the man shouts, staring at the torn leash. "It just snapped."

I run over to the dog and kneel down to check if she's still alive. The blood flowing from her face runs down the sloped road, disappearing under the car. I can see there's a lot of it, too much to leave any doubt about the dog's fate, but I press my hand against the pup's chest anyway. It's warm, but there is no movement, no heartbeat. The remnant of the tattered leash lies limp across the dog's body, still attached to her collar. A couple rhinestones have popped free, shining as they lay caught in the dirty hair of her neck. Attached to her collar is a silver tag engraved with her name: Gypsy.

The driver of the car opens her door to get out, but I wave her back. She doesn't need to see the mess her accident has caused. Not knowing what else to do, I take off my jacket and wrap Gypsy's body in it.

The man walks toward me then, hesitant, and he stumbles, nearly falling, when he misses the curb. I carry Gypsy to him. He cradles the bundle in shaking arms.

"It snapped. It just snapped," he says. Then without another word he turns and walks back up the hill. I walk back down.

When I reach the bottom of the hill and make the turn onto my own street, I glance back. The old woman's car hasn't moved.

Back at my house I go to the kitchen and grab a beer out of the fridge. I lean against the sink, staring out the window at my backyard, relishing the bitterness of the IPA. I keep thinking about the dog owner.

After a while, I dial my lawyer. "I think we should try again."

There's a long pause. I take another swig of beer.

"Do you mean the divorce settlement, or your marriage?" my lawyer asks.

I smile. "The marriage is toast," I say. "But she can have the damn boat."

After disconnecting, I think again about the dog owner. He is probably in his backyard digging a hole. I picture the pink collar around Gypsy's neck, the sunlight glittering on its fake jewels.

A wave of uncertainty fills me then, but the animosity I had felt earlier, that impelled me to take the walk, has vanished. I finish my beer in one long swallow.

It just snapped.

New River

Harlan Sr. has no interest in celebrating Thanksgiving—
or anything for that matter. Grumbling to himself
about turkeys and yams and dirty dishes, nothing but
nuisances to his thinking, he stares out the dining room's
large bay window at the view: across the flagstone patio
and the lawn beyond it, half-bare oaks line the bank of the
New River at the edge of his property. But he knows that
Ida, who is gone three months to the day, would be
disappointed in him if he didn't keep up the tradition. He
does it for her, he tells himself.

"Turkey's almost done, Mr. Gentry," Minnie says when
he steps into the kitchen.

Despite his reticence about the holiday, Harlan Sr. finds
the aroma of the roasting bird ambrosial. He stands for a
moment to pull it deep into his nostrils. Across the room
Minnie, his part-time housekeeper and cook, closes the
oven door after checking on the bird. Minnie has worked
for Harlan Sr. and Ida for forty-plus years, starting as a
nanny for Harlan Jr. and staying on long after the children
grew up and moved away. She is at least ten years older

than Harlan Sr. but, to his eyes, she hasn't aged a day in the past twenty years. Despite his insistence, Minnie has never called Harlan Sr. by his given name. To her, he is always "Mr. Gentry."

"Another twenty minutes and we can take this here tom out to cool a bit," Minnie says. "Then I'll heat up the corn casserole and those candied yams Miss Ida's friends cooked for y'all before I head home. Be a real nice feast, to be sure."

"Thank you, Minnie. I don't know what I'd have done without you. I never cooked a turkey in all my days."

Minnie laughs and nods. "Had no need to. Miss Ida was one of the finest cooks I ever known."

For a few moments, neither speaks. Minnie turns to unwrap the aluminum foil from the baking dishes the neighbors had dropped off for Harlan Sr. that morning.

"Sure be nice to have the children back in the house, won't it, Mr. Gentry?" Minnie says, placing a baking dish on the stovetop. "A house just ain't a home without children in it."

"I suppose." Harlan Sr. considers the presence of Junior and Ellen on the first Thanksgiving without their mother.

He pats the pockets of his cardigan, searching for his pipe. The children, especially Ellen, hate his smoking habit, and chide him whenever they see him doing so. He'd better enjoy it before they arrive.

At the door to his study, Harlan Sr. stops abruptly. He could have sworn that he heard—as he has so many times in the past sixty years—the swift crack of breaking china. When he was a child, living just two hours away in Winston-Salem, his father had been a lawyer at Reynolds Tobacco—back in the days when smoking was considered sophisticated rather than evil. Theirs was a comfortable life, and Harlan Sr. had wanted for little. But possessing creature comforts had not come without responsibilities. And wealth did not change the fact that actions had consequences. Both of these truths were lessons his father had insisted Harlan learn, and lessons he was more than willing to teach. As a boy, Harlan Sr. had often learned the hard way that chores assigned by his father were not to be forgotten or excused. Boundaries, too, needed to be understood. Privacy (his father's, that is) was at all costs to be respected. His father's study, for example, was never to be entered unless the old man was home and he had asked the boy to come in. The room was his father's fortress and retreat, and even Harlan's mother was seen entering the study only rarely. To the young Harlan this made it a dark and mysterious room. On the occasions when he was allowed in the room, the boy would stare at the two side walls, each fully lined with sleek, impressive law books and bedecked with photographs of his father standing with notable men of his time. The perpetual, heavy scent of cigar smoke hung thickly in the air, redolent of a sense of importance. Young Harlan knew instinctually there were unspoken and grave things said and decided there, imbuing this enigmatic place with a powerful and irresistible pull.

One Saturday night during the summer of Harlan Sr.'s tenth year, the temptation became too much. While his parents were occupied that evening at a social event, he gave in to his curiosity and crept into the study, hopeful of discovering some of his father's hidden secrets. While his memory of that calamitous night is hazy in many respects, his recollection of the moment he picked up the ornate dinner plate from a stand atop one of the bookcases will forever burn bright in his mind. Remembered distinctly, too, is the heft of the plate, an actual china piece from a White House state dinner that had been subsequently signed to Harlan Sr.'s father by President Roosevelt himself—and the split second it began to slip from Harlan's grasp and crash to the study floor. Harlan Sr., the boy, stood frozen at the paralyzing sound of the shattering dish, damaged beyond any attempt to repair it. For most children, the hours of agonizing waiting that followed would have been enough to learn the lesson that was, nonetheless, taught to Harlan later that evening with a perforated ash paddle applied with enough force to prevent the boy from sitting down for more than a week. A lesson Harlan Sr. has never forgotten.

Harlan Sr. checks his watch. It is already a few minutes past noon, the time his children were scheduled to arrive. Harlan Sr. furrows his already heavily wrinkled brow. Punctuality, he thinks somewhat ruefully, is no longer considered a virtue by his children's generation.

He shuffles into the living room and eases himself into the high back chair next to the window that faces the front of the house and the long, curved driveway. He picks up the newspaper Minnie had placed on the table next to the chair and glances at the depressing headlines but is in no mood to read any articles. Instead, as has become his habit in the past few months, Harlan Sr. looks around the room, registering all the objects—the cross-stitched pillows on the couch, the collection of ceramic birds perched along the mantelshelf, the myriad photographs taken of the family through the years—that are stark reminders of Ida's absence.

Noise from outside the window draws Harlan Sr. out of his reverie. Ellen's dark blue minivan is pulling up the driveway. Out of habit, he leans back, pressing his bony back against the cool leather of the chair to avoid being seen from outside. How many times had he done that, he wonders, late at night in the dark when the children were teenagers and had gone out for the evening with friends? Ida had chided him often for his suspicion and distrust of his own children, but hadn't he on more than one occasion seen his son slipping empty beer cans or liquor bottles from Harlan Sr.'s well-kept LTD and hiding them under his shirt well past the hour of his curfew? Or spied Ellen's vulgar dates groping clumsily underneath her blouse when she kissed them good night? Ida had been a smart woman but was in many things—mostly regarding her own children—too trusting and naive. It had fallen to Harlan Sr. to bear the brunt of disciplining them.

Ellen emerges from the van and walks around the front, stopping to look toward the window where her father watches, staring for a moment before shaking her head. Harlan Sr. snaps his head farther against the chair back and feels his cheeks flush. He scolds himself for such foolish behavior and leans forward again to peer out the window. Ellen is sliding the large side door open and stands facing the van, gesticulating as she speaks. Harlan Sr. gazes out the window for several minutes, considering whether he should go outside to help her or stay put. He watches Ellen's hands fly about as she talks to her boys. At one point, she throws them up in the air, a gesture he's seen her make since she was a little girl and an indication that what she's attempting is futile. Harlan Sr. finds it hard not to smile, hoping his daughter at last may understand the trials of child-rearing. More than once, Harlan Sr. sees his daughter throw a glance over her shoulder in his direction, but he's confident he is out of view.

Ellen moves toward the van's rear as her twins, Jacob and Jackson, emerge from the side. The boys are tall and lanky (wormy is how Harlan Sr. thinks of them) and their movements languorous as they climb out. They stand slouching beside the van until it is obvious their mother calls to them to help her at the back of the car. Ellen had been tasked with bringing dessert and Harlan Sr. imagines her stopping at the Food Lion a few blocks over to purchase pre-packaged pies of some sort.

Just as Ellen hands the Tupperware containers containing the desserts to her sons and slams down the hatch, Junior's big SUV turns into the driveway and parks behind her van. Harlan Sr. watches as his oldest child and Joni, his new daughter-in-law and Junior's third wife, step out of the vehicle. Ellen hurries over to hug her brother and sister-in-law. A few words are shared and the three of them look toward the house, specifically at the window from which Harlan Sr. is observing them, and they all begin to laugh. Harlan Sr. again feels heat rise in his cheeks. He pushes himself up from his chair, bracing for the sharp burst of fire he knows he'll feel in his knees as he takes the first couple steps, and crosses the living room to the foyer. He pauses to catch his breath and to glance at the grandfather clock standing guard in the short hallway by the front door. The encased pendulum swings in its fixed rhythm, the slight echo of its tick-tocking bringing a familiar comfort to Harlan Sr., and he has a sudden desire to stand there all day. But the front door opens and the abrupt brightness of the daylight invading the dimly lit foyer causes Harlan Sr. to squint.

"Hello, Father. The turkey sure smells great," Ellen says. She steps forward, giving Harlan Sr. a quick, light hug before moving past him to allow the others to enter, and before the old man can even lift his arms halfway to return the hug.

Jacob and Jackson follow, nodding to their grandfather in turn, hoisting the boxes of dessert as though they were a tribute to a tribal elder.

"Happy Thanksgiving, boys," Harlan Sr. says, but they've already moved toward the back of the house.

Harlan Sr. peers out the open door to watch Junior and his new family making their way up the brick walkway. Joni is pushing a stroller whose seat contains a large quilted diaper bag, while her husband carries baby Noah in a car seat dangling by his side.

"Happy Thanksgiving, sir," Junior says, reaching the front door and extending his free hand for a handshake.

"Same to you, son," the elder man responds.

The two shake hands and Harlan Sr., who has always felt you can judge a man by the firmness of his handshake, hates that his own son's grip seems flimsy and unsure.

Joni enters and gives her father-in-law a kiss on the cheek before offering her own wish of a happy holiday. Harlan Sr. is surprised by the gesture, able only to nod in response.

A loud squeal from behind him causes Harlan Sr. to turn. Minnie has come from the kitchen and is squeezing Ellen in a robust grip.

"Lawdy, girl, you have lost too much weight," Minnie says. "Those boys of yours must eat everything before you can even snatch a bite for yourself. Now where are those two scoundrels?"

Harlan Sr. watches as Ellen turns aside and allows Minnie to hug Jackson and Jacob, who smile and give the old woman a kiss, one on each cheek.

"You boys minding your mother?" Minnie asks. "'Cause if you ain't, you know ol' Minnie still got enough sting to give you both a whoopin'."

They all begin laughing and the twins both say in unison, "Yes, ma'am."

"Now, where's my Junior?" Minnie says, tilting her head to look beyond Ellen toward the door.

"Here I am, Minnie," Junior says and steps around his father to go to her.

Junior and Minnie embrace. "You look as beautiful as ever, Minnie," he says after they pull apart.

Minnie slaps Junior lightly on the arm. "Oh, you ol' flatterer. You never change."

Harlan Sr. stands in the open doorway watching as Minnie greets his children and their families, ending with effusive fussing over baby Noah. The group, laughing and chatting, move farther inside the house. Harlan Sr. stays in the doorway, listening as the sound of their prattle becomes an indistinct murmur.

A cold breeze pushes into the house, sending a shiver through Harlan Sr. and breaking the inertia in which he's found himself. He starts to close the front door but as he does he glances out at Ellen's minivan. In spite of the chill air, Harlan Sr. stands gazing at the vehicle until his eyes no longer register the bulky van but convey to his mind a tan station wagon with a sizable dent in the passenger side door belonging to Rodney Pegram, the shiftless worm who Ellen had dated her freshman year in high school.

It was that time—Harlan Sr. grimaces and closes his eyes at the memory but cannot stop its advance—when he watched that car from the living room window, the engine idling long after it had parked. At last the chubby Rodney, his acne so abundant it is readily visible in the dim porch light filtering across the driveway, comes around in false gallantry to open the car door for Ellen to get out. The two of them, Ellen and Rodney, embrace and kiss until Harlan Sr. notices Rodney's left hand slide underneath Ellen's pale blue blouse. Harlan Sr. sees the blouse's material bunching on Rodney's wrist as he moves it upward to latch on to his daughter's breast. The exposed skin of Ellen's belly seems almost to glow in the reflected house light and this, more than anything, impels Harlan Sr. to action. He thrusts the front door open, vaguely cognizant of the sound of it striking against the wall where it will leave a depression that remains unrepaired for two months, charges outside, and grabbing the surprised teenager by his shoulders, heaves him across the hood of the station wagon. Looming over the panicky boy, Harlan Sr. repeatedly slaps Rodney's face hard enough for Harlan Sr. to rupture a blood vessel in his finger and cause a painful hematoma that remains for more than a week. All this time he is screaming at the boy: "Get the hell off my property, you filthy punk. If I catch you near my daughter again, I swear I will put you in the hospital." And then, even as Ellen is tugging his sleeve and yelling for him to stop, Harlan Sr. raises his fist to strike Ellen's date the decisive blow. He is burning with an uncontrolled rage and his arm begins to arc down. Harlan Sr.'s arm is stopped short, however, when Junior, who'd heard the commotion and run outside, grabs his father's arm and pulls Harlan Sr. back, away from the car.

The revulsion Harlan Sr. saw in his son's eyes was plain as the younger shouted, "It's bad enough you always bully your own children, but to pick on someone else's is pathetic even by your standards. You disgust me." Harlan Sr.—confused, angry, embarrassed by the outburst—began to reprimand his son for speaking to him that way, particularly in front of Rodney, but instead walked back into the house, past Ida, whose shaking hands covered her face. Harlan Sr. went to his study where he closed and locked the door and stayed sitting, alone and awake, until the following morning.

After finally shutting the front door, Harlan Sr. stays in the foyer, letting the house's warmth remove the chill from him. Ellen's faint voice, as well as Junior's and Joni's and the twins', can be heard coming from the kitchen. He turns his head in an effort to hear what they are saying. His hearing has deteriorated, however, and their words are muffled. Interspersed between the sounds of chatter, a quick burst of laughter erupts and Harlan Sr. somehow knows they are laughing at him. As he continues listening to the indistinct voices he becomes certain of it. Always, he thinks bitterly, he has had to bear the burden of being the one who forsook popularity in order to teach through discipline. Ida was soft and too doting, so the task had fallen upon him, and not by his own choosing. It is a father's duty. Harlan Sr. knows that well enough. Yet have his children ever had the insight to understand the weight of that responsibility? Not once, by his reckoning. In fact, they return his caring with venomous words and avoidance. Harlan Sr. stands trembling in the foyer, fighting the resentment that is building within him, wishing he'd never insisted on continuing this wretched holiday tradition that Ida alone had loved.

Harlan Sr. strides into the kitchen where the suddenness of his appearance causes the others to stop talking. Junior lifts the large turkey out of the oven and places it on the stovetop to cool. Minnie, who'd been buttoning her coat, stops and looks along with the others at Harlan Sr. The old man's face flushes red as he takes them all in with a wild look that confuses and unsettles them.

After a moment of awkward silence, Junior says, "Father, doesn't the turkey look wonderful?" He points to the crisp, brown bird.

"Ingrates!" Harlan Sr. shouts. "Not once have any of you children so much as said thank you to me. Is a little gratitude too much to ask after all these years?"

"Dad, what are you talking about?" Ellen says. "Junior simply asked if you liked the turkey."

Harlan Sr. stares at his daughter for a moment then turns to regard the turkey sitting in the roast pan atop the stove as if he is seeing it for the first time. He walks over to it. As he does, Joni, Ellen, Jackson, and Jacob step back in turn, as though Harlan Sr. is Moses and they the Red Sea. Harlan Sr. looks down at the turkey, the aroma strong but no longer pleasant to him, then takes his arm and sweeps the entire pan off the stovetop. Grease and juice splatter the floor, as well as the legs of Junior's pants.

"That's what I think of your damned turkey," Harlan Sr. says. "*Now* how does it look?" The old man turns and walks out of the kitchen, slipping a bit in the oily mess on the floor. Noah, now in his stroller, begins to wail.

Harlan Sr. goes first into the living room where he snatches a framed photograph of Ida and himself taken on their wedding day. The image is faded and slightly out of focus, but it's the only remaining picture from that day. He takes the photo and retreats to his study, slamming the door behind him. He plops into a chair arranged by the window. Harlan Sr.'s breaths are raspy and rapid. He gazes at the photograph, at his younger, happier self, and marvels at how ignorant to the harsh cruelties of the world that boy was. He can hear the sound of footsteps approaching outside in the hallway, along with the hushed voices of his children and grandchildren. There is a tentative knock on the door. Ellen calls through it, beseeching him to come out. Harlan Sr. ignores her, much the way, he figures, she and her brother have done with him over the years. With a wry but cheerless smile he turns then to look out the window, which like the one in the dining room, faces the backyard. Harlan Sr. looks off toward where the lawn drops down to the New River beyond the oak trees. Although he can't see it, he imagines the water beneath the leaden sky, rough and choppy as it flows north. From out in the hall, Junior's voice joins Ellen's in pleading with him to open the door. But Harlan Sr. pays no attention to them. Instead, still staring toward the river, he rubs his bony fingers across the smooth glass of the picture frame and whispers, "Ida. . .Ida. . .Ida."

Life List

I was surprised to find Teresa already in the kitchen, pouring water into the coffeemaker. I glanced out the window that overlooks the backyard. In the nebulous predawn light, the trees were barely visible, more the suggestion of trees than actual ones.

"Wow, you're up before the sun on a Saturday," I said. "Couldn't sleep?"

Teresa didn't turn or look at me. She scooped coffee into a filter. "I've got a lot to do this morning."

"Like what?"

"A pet adoption fair this afternoon. I told the director I'd help get everything set up."

"You certainly have become a busy bee."

Teresa, usually a homebody whom I have teased many times about bordering on agoraphobic, had recently become involved in several activities outside the home. In the past ten months she'd joined a biweekly book club, helped deliver meals to seniors, and volunteered for a local animal rescue group.

"Besides, I thought you said you were going bird-watching this morning?" she said.

"Birding."

"What?"

"It's called birding," I said. "'Bird-watching' is looking *at* birds. Birders go and look *for* birds."

"Well, excuse me."

I walked over to the cupboard to retrieve my thermos, whose lining is coffee-dyed from years of use.

"And I might not be home for dinner," Teresa said.

"Why? Do people adopt pets at night now?"

"No, smartass. But there's cleaning up, paperwork, things you wouldn't know about. In any event, I'll probably be late, so while you're out you might want to grab something to fix for dinner."

"It's getting so those shut-ins you deliver meals to have dinner with you more often than I do."

Teresa looked at me then, frowning. "All those years you complained I never left the house and now that I have interests, you complain."

"I'm not complaining," I said. "I'm just not used to it, is all. Besides, it's the weekend and I was thinking we might have dinner at Bernardin's. We haven't been there in ages."

She looked at me for a moment and didn't say anything, but then she nodded and turned away. "I'm going up to get dressed. I hope you have fun and see lots of birds."

I watched her walk out of the kitchen. The room was still except for the gurgle and drip of the coffeemaker. I thought about when Teresa and I met twenty-eight years ago. Back then I often spent my free time in the woods and fields of the North Carolina Piedmont. I'd become adept at identifying even distant birds by only a faint snippet of a song or call. Teresa, who never had any particular interest in the hobby, had seemed enamored of the bookish seriousness with which I pursued my pastime. It was a large part, I'd always thought, of what drew her to me. But as the years evaporated and our lives picked up the tedious rhythm most marriages achieve, our time became filled with prosaic needs—jobs, bills, and all the banal requirements of everyday survival. With no children in our lives to provide the shared burden and bond that parenthood brings, we'd come not so much to live together as exist together.

I headed to the den to gather my things: knapsack with frayed straps, twenty-year-old Swarovski binoculars with lenses as crystal clear as the day I bought them, my creased and dog-eared field guide, my lucky ball cap I credit for many first sightings. On my way back to the kitchen to fill my thermos, I heard the shower running upstairs and Teresa singing.

After I filled my thermos and stuffed a Ziploc to stretching with pretzels, I headed for the kitchen door. Teresa's pocketbook was on the counter and I noticed a scrap of paper jutting out from underneath it. It was a store receipt, on the back of which she'd scribbled a grocery list. On a whim, I snatched up the list and shoved it into my pants pocket, figuring I'd save her the errand when I stopped at the store on the way home that afternoon.

As I drove along empty roads toward the park, the newly greened trees stood silent in the gauzy dawn light, watching me it seemed. I powered down the car window to let cool air rush against my bare face. I figured by the time I arrived at the park in another hour, the sun would be just rising above the horizon, and the air would start to warm. When I pulled up at a stop sign before turning onto the county road that leads to the park's entrance, the mingling songs of the dawn chorus immersed the car's cabin, lifting my spirits, exciting me with anticipation. The spring songbird migration was near its peak, and I'd hoped to add to my extensive list of sightings. Perhaps my first Philadelphia Vireo or Connecticut Warbler, rarities in North Carolina that I'd read had been spotted in the nearby foothills.

In my brightened mood, I summoned the memory of driving along the very same road one evening many years before, when Teresa and I had been married less than a year. We were heading to a Christmas party hosted by her boss, who owned the small podiatrist's office where she was the receptionist. Teresa was dressed in a dazzling, tight red dress. Neither of us had been able to keep our hands from caressing the other's legs as I drove, and by the time we were only a few blocks from the podiatrist's home, I pulled the car off onto a darkened side street where in short order we were in the back seat grappling in a tangle of hastily removed clothing and slick limbs.

It was hard not to smile when I remembered we never made it to the party. But my smile faded quickly. It had been a long while since Teresa and I kissed in any way. How long *had* it been, I wondered as I made the turn onto the narrow county road, since Teresa and I shared the singular electricity of holding our naked selves against each other? Or delighted in the slippery pleasure so common in those early days of our marriage?

Twenty minutes later, movement on my left drew my attention and I spotted a pair of crows silhouetted against the roseate sky. I found their strident caws pleasurable. It was 6:50 when I slowed the car at the state park's entrance gate. I saw a ranger shuck off his jacket and dump it into the backseat of his vehicle. He tossed a quick wave in my direction. I drove up to the padlocked barricade and lowered the passenger window. The park ranger, a young man, whom I pegged at no older than twenty-five, leaned down and flicked the brim of his campaign hat back from his face.

"Good morning, sir."

"Sure is."

"Looking to take an early morning hike?"

I lifted the knapsack resting on the passenger seat. "Gonna do a little birding. Hope to add to my life list."

"Well, your timing's perfect. I've seen quite a few migrants in the past week." The ranger pointed to a line of chokeberry shrubs edging the entrance road, just past the barrier. "There are a number of redstarts hanging around right over in that thicket near the parking area.

I glanced where the ranger pointed and nodded.

"The park doesn't open for another ten minutes, sir," the ranger said. "But. . .I'm going to make an executive decision. Hang on a sec."

I watched the ranger jiggle a ring of keys he took from his pocket. He then unlatched the padlock securing the bar blocking the park's entrance road. He swung the fulcrum and signaled for me to drive forward. I eased off the brake, tossed a quick two-fingered salute in the young man's direction. I drove up to the parking area and chose a space from the empty lot closest to the main trailhead. I threw my cell phone into the glove compartment before grabbing my binoculars and knapsack. I got out and stood quietly for a moment, all alone in the still, peaceful morning. I hooked the strap of the field glasses around my neck and breathed deeply. The air brimmed with fecundity, saturated with the spring scents of new life. The brightening sky held only scattered shreds of clouds. Somewhere to my right, beyond the trailhead, I heard the choked gurgle of a rock-strewn creek.

And everywhere around me, there were the songs of birds.

I stripped off my sweater and left it in the car. For the first hour or so within the lush confines of the forest, the air would still be clutching the remains of the night's chill, but I knew as the sun crested the upper limits of the canopy, the day would warm comfortably. I hoisted my pack onto my back, jigging the straps snugly across my shoulders. My field guide was at the ready behind my back, tucked in the waistband of my pants.

Walking toward the trail, I studied the hedge line along the road. Immediately, I caught a flitting movement and lifted the binoculars, training them on the bush. A series of sweet, high-pitched notes emanated just before a male redstart popped into view in a gap among the leaves. I made fine adjustments to the focus wheel, admiring the beauty of the bird's brilliant orange shoulder patches and wing bars before the bird darted away. Immediately to his left, a hooded warbler sharply voiced its distinctive call. It didn't take me long to find the bold black and yellow bird and hold it in my gaze until the migrant hopped from view. I lowered my binoculars and started again for the trail. By habit, I tilted my neck back and scanned the pale expanse of the morning sky. Directly above, a brace of red-tailed hawks glided along in nimble, unhurried loops. Having taken no more than a couple steps, I noted I had identified three species. I smiled, sensing this boded well for a gratifying day of sightings. I decided to start a list, not trusting my increasingly unreliable memory. From a flapped pocket on the side of my pack I retrieved a pen, but I was momentarily confused when the small notebook, which I habitually carry to record my observations, was not there. I rummaged through the main compartment with no luck. All at once, I remembered taking the book out several days before in order to review my list from previous years' migrations, leaving it on the desk in my den.

I considered retrieving my cell phone to record my sightings, like many modern birders do, but I found it distracting and clumsy, and hated the interruptions from calls and texts. When I shoved my hand in my pockets, searching for anything upon which to scribble notes, my left hand found the crumpled store receipt with Teresa's shopping list. Not a lot of room to write, but I could abbreviate.

Teresa's precise cursive nearly filled the entire space on the back of the receipt. I flipped it over to see if there was any room on the printed side that I could use. At first, my eyes registered only the blank margins, making a quick assessment of their utility for my purpose. But instinctively, I read the printing on the receipt, which I noticed was from the local Walgreen's pharmacy. There was only one purchased item listed. When I read it I looked up, blinking and confused, and glanced back to where I'd spotted the hooded warbler, as if I could rewind time to erase the error of my misreading. In the sharp, crystalline light of the new day, I read again the item line on the printout:

EPT PREGNANCY TEST 2 COUNT $14.95

Who, I wondered, would Teresa be buying pregnancy tests for? I stared at the sale slip, the words blurring as my vision turned inward to see my wife in the budding days of our marriage. Teresa was tugging at my clothes, yanking my shirttails free, stripping off my trousers in frenzied desire, shoving me onto the bed or sofa or carpet at all hours of the day before mounting me. I readily remembered the taut softness of her youthful skin as I clenched her waist, my fingertips registering the tensing of the muscles of her back as she arched backward in the final ecstasy of the moment. She would collapse beside me, the sheen of sweat on her neck, a satisfied grin on her face. I remembered the confidence in her voice, so certain that was the time that had worked. A hope invariably dashed. Until eventually, despite test after test assuring us we should be able to conceive, the last atom of optimism drained from my wife's heart, and she accepted the bitter reality that her and my journey together would be ours alone.

I stood in the wide, empty parking lot, staring at my solitary car, confused. In the downy light I eyed the store receipt like an Egyptologist deciphering obscure hieroglyphics. There were, I told myself, many potential explanations for this mystery. My mind enumerated them (all the while repelling the one prickly concern pushing its way to the front of my thoughts)—the receipt was not Teresa's, but one she found littering a sidewalk and felt it her civic duty to pick up; the purchase was for a friend to whom Teresa had mentioned she'd be out shopping; it was an improperly scanned bar code of a different item she had purchased. I struggled to think of more options. Then, ceding at last to the unthinkable, there was the possibility that there *was* no mistake, and my wife needed to know if she was pregnant.

The air, which had moments before filled my nose and lungs with the pleasant thrill of springtime, now felt thick and heavy—nearly unbreathable. I squeezed the shred of paper into a tight ball in my fist and thrust it back into my pocket. I took one step back toward the car, knowing I should go home and clear up the mystery, but I stopped. Instead, I moved toward the trailhead, my steps short, leaden, as though my ankles were hobbled. Around me, the exalted melodies of a dozen or more birds, proclaiming their territories or wooing mates, were lost in the howl of blood in my ears. My concentration severed, I shuffled along the path, oblivious now to the bounteous natural activity in the surrounding woods that I had come seeking.

A half mile along, there was a sharp bend in the main path as it veered abruptly away from the nearby creek. The emphatic burble of the stream held me entranced and, for a moment, I was distracted from my unease. I threaded my way through the thicket in the water's direction. My boots snagged in the vined underbrush, and I had to jerk my feet violently to free them. Just beyond the border of trees, I came to the narrow hem of damp earth that edged the noisy creek. Not far downstream, I spotted the fallen trunk of a broad oak whose top half had snapped off and was dragged away by the current. The spiked crown of the remaining stump rested beyond the bank, the tip barely submerged, pushing large, jagged points just below the surface, which caused the water to eddy and churn.

The thick rubber bottoms of my boots sank into the soft, grayish loam, leaving a trail of perfect casts of my soles when I headed to sit on the stump. It was cooler down by the water, and I felt the muted pinpricks as goosebumps rose on my bare forearms. I rubbed them distractedly. Nearby, a Louisiana Waterthrush whistled and bobbed its tail in the shallow mud. As I settled onto the tree trunk, the book wedged in the back of my chinos dug into the small of my back, but I made no move to retrieve it. I let my eyes settle on the place in the stream where the water labored to rush past the enormous spikes at the tree's severed end. I studied how it splashed across the hardwood, sounding like rapid, impotent slaps, as though the water was rebuking this unwelcome intruder.

My heartbeats mounted perceptibly as conversations with Teresa from the past year were recalled with enhanced clarity.

Your book club ran late.

Oh, you know. It was as much the Chardonnay as the discussion about the book.

Which book this time?

Nothing you'd ever read. A girly thing with lots of romance.

Do all the ladies dress up, too?

Women like to look nice.

Then, from just that morning:

And I might not be home for dinner.

In any event, I'll probably be late, so you might want to grab something to fix for dinner.

I wondered, too, about the evenings when I'd arrived home from work to an empty house, only to find a note saying she'd be stuck at a volunteers' meeting with the director of the animal shelter and that perhaps I should order a pizza. And hadn't I remarked, just last week, how much more my wife was smiling? I'd ascribed it to her enjoying her newfound avocations.

My shoulders sagged. Close by, a woodpecker drummed repeatedly in hope of dislodging some insect or extracting a bit of sap. A thinly leafed branch floated by in the current. The incessant purling of the stream tripping over the fallen tree hypnotized me, and I remained still, as though I was a part of the log on which I sat, an anomalous growth sprouting from the trunk. Soon, I became aware of nothing save the mad pulsing of blood behind my eyes.

The sun rose high. My back ached from the ceaseless hunching posture I had assumed. A great blue heron emerged from its shoreline hiding spot across the creek and stealthily skimmed the water's surface until it disappeared from my sightline. I didn't bother to hoist my binoculars. I kept telling myself I should drive home and simply ask Teresa about the receipt. But, I wondered, had enough distrust already permeated my heart that I would believe whatever she claimed?

It was not quite ten o'clock when I decided to leave. Stippled sunlight freckled the ground of the woods as I maneuvered back between the pines and oaks toward the main trail. Once on the path, I hesitated, looking from one direction to the other—deeper into the woods, to the familiar and comforting forest, or back to my car, which would take me home, to the unknown. I plodded along, away from the park's entrance, and headed deeper into the woods. I knew I'd missed the best shot of seeing many birds, as they had settled in during the warmth of the day after a busy morning of moving about, foraging and building nests. There were more people in the park then and I nodded silent greetings when they passed me or I raised my binoculars in pretense at studying some bird in order to avoid contact entirely.

Despite my riven mood, I managed to identify dozens of birds over the next two hours. When I came upon the base of a tall pine abutting the path, I noticed a large patch of chalky white splotches and gazed up to discover a nest lodged in the high, tangled branches. Just visible with the binoculars, above the nest's edge, was the distinctive head of a yellow-crowned night heron, the long trailing feathers of its eponymous crown bobbing in the soft breeze of the treetop. I stepped off the path onto the bed of pine needles at the side of the tree in order to get a better sightline on the bird. With my eyes trained upward, I felt my foot press down on a spongy lump and jumped backward. Lying on the tree litter was a dead hatchling. I stared at the bulbous blue-black eyelids and the ragged new feathers that sprouted from the chick's drying, dimpled skin.

I peered up at the nest before crouching next to the dead bird. Using curled fingers, I scraped a narrow grave beside where it lay. I nudged the diminutive carcass into the hole with the tip of one boot, shoveling dirt and needles on top of it with the sides of my foot.

Finding the dead heron had sucked all my will to continue looking for birds, so I decided to head home at last to face what I'd been avoiding. The midday warmth had drawn out raw, earthy scents from the trees and land. As I retraced my trek, I welcomed the return of the creek's song, building as I neared the final bend of the path close to the trail's entrance. The raucous sound of teenage boys laughing and talking loudly broke the spell I was in, and soon I spied a trio of them ahead on the road. As they passed by, one of the boys asked if I'd found anything good, gesturing to the binoculars. I gave a noncommittal shrug, but the boys had already moved past me, not truly interested in any answer.

I approached the trailhead and paused in the last trace of shade where the trees ended before giving way to the sun-

soaked clearing of the full parking lot. I stood contemplating
Teresa's answers that awaited me. But at that moment, I
was surrounded only by the unspoken disinterest of the
forest. All at once, from close behind me, a red-eyed vireo
repeated its jeering, undulating call, easily identified by a
common mnemonic: *Here I am; Where are you? Here I am;
Where are you?* I stared at my feet, and my eyes settled on
the dirt smudges from burying the dead chick. I listened for
several minutes to the vireo's persistent song. *Here I am;
Where are you? Here I am; Where are you?*

I retrieved the balled-up Walgreen's receipt from my
pocket and held it in my open palm and stared at it. I
knew it was no more than a fraction of an ounce, but I felt
the weight of it on my hand. I closed my eyes and once
again envisioned Teresa naked, her back arched as she
climaxed, but the memory was no longer a happy one.
Weariness engulfed me then. I opened my eyes, looked
briefly at the receipt and then tossed it into the woods. I
turned and headed back into the wilderness, and I walked
until I found a small spoor that tracked deep into the woods
in a part of the park I'd never explored. The vireo continued
to call. *Here I am; Where are you? Here I am; Where are
you?* I followed it, deeper and deeper into the forest, until
I found the elusive bird resting on a branch of a tall pine.
He stayed there a long while. I sat on the cool ground and
watched him.

"Here I am," I whispered to the vireo. "Here I am."

Secret Santa Gift

My elf flashes three fingers at me. Just three more snot-dripping brats and I can collect my fifty bucks and escape the jarring holiday cheer of this mall. Normally, I'd take my cash straight to the liquor store for a half pint of Crown, but it's Christmas Eve and I haven't gotten my old lady a gift yet. Not that she deserves squat the way she's on my case all the time, but if I don't get her something I'll regret it in that way only married men can understand.

Brittany leads a boy toward me who looks to be about five and I check the crotch of his pants for signs of pee, because, let's face it, Santa doesn't like getting his legs wet. I glance then at Brittany, a high school senior who works the camera part-time, and I smile. She's just a kid and I hate myself—a little anyway—for thinking how hot she looks in that little elf costume.

"Here you go, Devon," Brittany says, "up onto Santa's lap."

The boy looks up at me, both nervous and excited, and Brittany sticks her tongue out at him behind his back. I grin and try to get into character. As Brittany heads back to her station it's all I can do to drag my eyes off her ass and focus on little Devon.

"So, Devon, what do you want for Christmas," I say.

"Wow, you know my name?"

It happens dozens of times a day. The little farts are so excited about seeing Santa Claus that they don't hear my elf say their name when they come up to my chair.

"Of course I do, Devon. Santa knows the names of all the boys and girls in the world."

"Wow."

His excitement is real and I get a flutter of fear he'll be a leaker.

"So what do you want me to bring to your house this year?"

I blink as Brittany flashes the camera. Devon's whiny voice rattles off the useless crap he hopes I'll bring him, but won't. My mind wanders. For some dumbass reason, the mall management put Santa's Workshop right next to the food court, and a sickening odor wafts past us. Whoever thought it was a good idea to position a Chik-fil-A, a Jade Wok, and a Sbarro's next to each other should be duct taped to a very hard chair and forced to smell their combined aromas for four straight hours. Without the $12.50 an hour.

I sense a silence and realize Devon has stopped talking.

"Well, have you been a good boy this year?" I ask. Devon nods furiously, frantic enough for me to know he's lying. Good thing I don't give a shit. "Then I'll see what I can do. You behave and do what your mom and dad say, okay?"

Again he nods and this time I join him. That's my signal for Brittany to come and rescue me. She strolls over and leads Devon back to his smiling, proud mother, who just shelled out $19.50 for a 5x7 glossy of Devon with dear ol' Santa.

After the last of the morning lot of kids, Brittany strings the velvet rope across our area and adjusts the sign dangling from it that announces that Santa had to go feed his reindeer.

It *should* say that Santa had to go drain his weasel, but I don't expect the mall manager would allow that.

I wave bye to Brittany, sneaking one last peek at her ass.

"See you tomorrow, Jolly Saint Dick," she says and I laugh.

I hurry toward the hallway that leads to the lockers, grinning at the idiots streaming past me in their quest to throw their money away. After turning in my scratchy costume and collecting my fifty bucks, I start thinking about a present to get my wife. Since I'm already here at the mall, I consider grabbing something quick. I debate a pair of shades at the Sunglasses Hut versus an airbrushed license plate made with her name, Della, which she could put on the front of her Saturn. In the end, though, I decide to get the hell out of the mall with its crazed shoppers and funky food smells and drive downtown.

It's cold and raining when I cross the packed parking lot to the staff area. I start my car and wait for the heater to kick in. My body heat steams up the windshield and I have to swipe it with my sleeve so I can see out. After a few minutes of shivering, I give up on the heat and pull away.

There's a variety store downtown—what we called a five-and-dime when I was a kid—just around the corner from the liquor store I usually go to, so I decide to head there. Traffic near the mall is a bitch, but once I go a few blocks it clears up. On the way, I ponder gifts for Della. Last year, she was on one of her frequent and futile diets, so I found her a nice, fancy scale that not only tells her weight, but her body mass index, her bone density, her heart rate, and more. I was trying to be encouraging and to show Della I cared, but she just started crying when she opened it, saying it meant I thought she was fat. This led to her informing me, as she does every year, that I've ruined Christmas again. Then the annual holiday bawling commenced, followed by her ranting about how she hates this time of year because Christmas is for kids and we could never have kids and it always ends up somehow being my fault. Honestly, I don't know why I try.

Christmas wasn't always so fucked up for us. The first few years we were married, we lived in a tiny efficiency apartment just across the railroad tracks east of town. In the winter, the radiator either didn't work at all, making the joint so cold we could see our breath, or it wouldn't shut off, making the place as hot as a sauna. Della and I would either sit on the couch in our coats or walk around naked, unashamed of our bodies the way young people are. We never had extra money for the holiday, but somehow Della managed to pull together scraps of cloth and paper and decorate the place really nice. Christmas Eve, I'd come home from work and walk in and she'd have put on the Dean Martin Christmas Album—her favorite— the apartment smelling great from a chicken she was roasting. Della would be nowhere in sight, so I'd call her name and then she'd step out of the bathroom wearing nothing but a big ribbon angled across her body, a huge bow strategically arranged between her legs. Then she'd ask if I wanted to open my present right then or wait until after dinner. Seems like we always ate burnt chicken on Christmas Eve.

But ten, then fifteen, then twenty years passed, we moved into a bigger apartment, we both gained weight, and Christmas was never the same.

I still have no idea what to get Della by the time I reach Liberty Street. I circle the block three times before I notice an SUV pulling away from the curb. I snag the spot and by the time I get out of the car the rain has picked up. It also feels like the temperature has dropped ten degrees since I left the mall. I check the parking meter and see there's about twenty minutes left. At least one thing goes my way today. That ought to be plenty of time to find something. Surely, a quick pass up and down the aisles of Dingle's Variety will reveal just the right gift for Della. And if I'm lucky, I'll have enough dough left over so that I can run around the block to the liquor store.

I step inside Dingle's, letting the nice, heated air warm me, then check my watch to calculate my departure time to avoid a parking ticket. I amble up the aisle on the far right, but there's nothing but cleaning supplies and pet food. Weaving up and down the rest of the aisles I pick up and consider several items—a bottle of something called "eau de toilette," which I guess is some type of cologne because it's with all the other perfumes, but I put it back because Della will just think I'm telling her she smells bad; some fancy soaps shaped like seashells, passed over for the same reason; a briefly considered T-shirt with the words "World's Greatest Wife" written in large, glittery script, but she'd need an extra large and I didn't have to think very long about the shit storm that would occur if I went home with that. In the end, I settle on a pair of thick, fuzzy socks she can wear around the house and the largest Chia pet they have, which is a bust of Elvis.

The wind has picked up when I step outside, and the rain blows in my face. Since I managed to come in well below budget on Della's gifts, I decide to head around the corner to reward myself with some Crown Royal. Halfway down the block I duck into a narrow alleyway to get out of the biting wind and to light a cigarette. I stuff the bag with Della's presents under my arm and try to dig into my jeans pocket with cold, stiff fingers to retrieve my lighter. A slight movement to my right catches my eye. At first I don't see anything. Just a row of garbage cans, so I figure it must've been a rat or a cat. I'm just about to look away when I notice the lid of the nearest garbage can wiggle. Certain now it's a rat, and being a little afraid of them, I decide to forget the cigarette and get on to the liquor store.

But as I turn, I hear a high-pitched noise that stops me. I look back at the trash can. The top is definitely jiggling, and after a few seconds, I hear the sound again. I walk over and reach for the lid's handle, ready to jump back in case an animal leaps out. I jerk the lid off and, even though nothing jumps out, I stumble back a step. The bag from Dingle's slips from my armpit and I hear Elvis break, but my eyes are fixed on the trash can.

Wrapped in damp, dirty newspapers is a baby.

The sudden exposure to cold air causes it to squirm and I watch its face turn deep red. It opens its mouth to cry but it doesn't seem to have enough air. Dropping the can lid, I step toward it. I glance back toward the sidewalk, hoping someone will walk by to help me, but no one does. I'm staring at the infant, contemplating how the hell it got there, afraid to touch it, when it finds its lungs and lets out a piercing wail. Instinctively, I pick up the baby and press it against my soggy windbreaker and start to rock back and forth. It stops crying. I touch the back of its head. The skin there is like ice, so I unzip my jacket and slide the baby inside, newspaper and all. I wonder how comforting my rapid heartbeat could possibly be.

I try to think of the fastest place to find a cop, and the old saw comes to mind about never seeing one when you need one and I realize how true it is. It occurs to me that the best place for this baby is the hospital, so I decide to take it there. When I start toward the sidewalk, I trip over the plastic bag I'd dropped and I nearly fall. I reach down to pick up Della's scattered presents when the idea comes to me.

Why not give Della something she has always wanted and be a hero at the same time?

By the time I get back to the apartment, my nerves are shot. I've wrapped the baby in an old sweater I found in the trunk of my car. It's pretty filthy, but I figured it was more important for it to be warm than clean. I laid the baby on the passenger seat of the car and drove with one hand on top of it and one hand on the steering wheel. When I got to our street, I had to park the car a half block from the front door to our building.

The rain has kept most people indoors, and I'm grateful. I check to see that no one is around and I tuck the baby into my jacket again. I grab the shopping bag from Dingle's, figuring it'll help me look more casual as I hurry into the apartment.

I walk up the two flights of stairs to our floor, the whole time feeling the infant shaking against my chest. Since I'm pressing the baby against me with one arm and holding the bag in the other, I can't get to my key. I kick the apartment door. After what seems forever I hear Della's footsteps on the other side.

"Who is it?"

"It's me, Della. Open up."

"For Christ's sake, did you forget your key again?"

"Come on, Della. Just open the door. It's kind of an emergency."

I hear the dead bolt clunk and the door opens. Della is standing in her bathrobe with her hand on her hip, a cigarette dangling from the corner of her mouth.

"How many times are you going to forget—"

I don't wait for her to finish. I push past her and shove the door closed with the back of my foot. Della, who'd been leaning on the door, nearly falls.

"You son of a bitch," she says.

I toss the Dingle's bag on the sofa and I turn toward Della, who is looking at me with that all-too-familiar look of disgust. I can see she's about to speak, but I hold my hand up to stop her.

"Just listen to me, Della, okay?"

"What's going on?" I see her eyes look down to where my arm is pressed against my jacket. "What's that under your coat?"

"Hear me out," I say, but just then the baby lets loose with another loud squall.

Like a scene from a lousy comedy, Della's mouth drops open and her cigarette falls onto the floor. For several moments, she doesn't move, doesn't even blink, so I walk over and stub out the butt. Then I unzip my jacket and hold the crying infant out to my wife. She reaches toward it and takes it from me. The baby is still crying, but Della cradles it in her arm and holds it against her breast. Just as I did earlier, she begins to rock and the baby quiets down but does not stop crying altogether. Della looks up at me and I can see the unspoken questions in her eyes.

I roll out the story for her about how I found it. . .and maybe embellish a little about how long I looked for a cop or someone to help me with it. It seems Della is only half listening to me, anyway. She keeps looking at the small, exposed part of the baby's head.

"Is it a boy or girl, Lou?"

"Shit. I don't know. I never looked."

Della walks over to the couch and eases the baby onto a cushion. She unfolds the sweater and then throws me a dirty look.

"Jesus Christ...you didn't even take the poor thing out of these dirty newspapers?"

Gingerly, she begins to unwrap the pages, but the damp newspaper just disintegrates. Della pulls it apart and the first thing I notice is not that the baby is a girl, but that there is a surprisingly long bit of umbilical cord snaking from the baby's belly. The cord and a good portion of the skin around it are discolored with brown, drying blood. I feel my pulse beating at my temples.

"Oh, Lord," Della says. "Lou, go call for an ambulance."

"But, Della, I thought we could—"

"Right now, Lou!"

I make the call and five minutes later I hear a siren approaching. While we wait, Della gets a blanket from the bedroom to wrap the little girl. She is sitting on the couch cooing to the infant when I hear the ambulance pull up outside.

The paramedics trot up the steps and I call down the stairs to guide them to our apartment. When they come over to Della and take the baby so they can examine it, I see that my wife has tears in her eyes and it hits me that I've managed to keep my streak intact. I have fucked up yet another Christmas.

Watching the EMTs stabilize the baby, I don't notice that a police officer has entered the apartment. When he touches me on the shoulder I jump. He asks me some questions, but says I need to show him where I found her and go to the station so he can fill out a full report. One of the paramedics picks up the girl and tells the officer he's heading over to Baptist Hospital.

The policeman asks Della a couple of quick questions— she doesn't know anything anyhow—and tells me we got to go. I look at Della, who is sitting in the same spot on the couch, and see that she is looking at me, shaking her head. Tears are running down her cheeks, but she makes no move to wipe them away.

"Listen, Della," I say, "I just thought that. . .well. . .I know you always wanted us to have a baby and it never quite worked out for us and all. . ."

"You're a jackass, Lou, you know that? A real damned jackass," Della says, but there's no meanness in her voice like I expect. "Go help the police officer and hurry home so we can have our Christmas."

I nod and turn to the cop. He indicates for me to go first and I start for the door. Before I head out, I turn and look once again at my wife. She is holding the blanket she'd wrapped the baby in against her face and crying soundlessly. She drops the blanket to her side and it covers most of the shopping bag from Dingle's.

"Hey," I say. "Don't look in that bag. Your presents are in there."

She looks again at the bag, and then at the blanket clutched in her hands. Without looking up she smiles and says, "Don't worry, Lou. Your secret is safe."

"Let's go, sir," the cop says.

I nod and walk out of the apartment. The policeman closes the door and we begin down the stairs. Before we get to the first landing I hear something that stops me. I tilt my head back up toward our floor and listen for a few seconds to be sure I'm hearing correctly. When I'm certain, I can't help but smile.

"What is it?" the cop asks.

"Don't you recognize that music?" I say. "That's Dean Martin, singing 'White Christmas.'"

Acknowledgments

It is with deepest thanks that I acknowledge those people who have helped to make *I Hear the Human Noise* a reality.

Special thanks goes to the talented writers in my monthly critique group—Joni Carter, Steve Lindahl, and Bob Shar—who helped shape these stories from sometimes bland and unsightly things to presentable works. I am forever grateful.

I also owe a debt to the editors of the fine journals and anthologies that published most of these stories. A writer's life is often filled with self-doubt and how much their belief in the merit of my work means cannot be overstated.

I am especially grateful to Claire V. Foxx at Press 53, whose hard work and eye for detail were an indispensable part of making this book happen.

Lastly, I'd like to thank my editor, Kevin Watson, whose encouragement, guidance, and, most of all, friendship, means more to me than I could ever express.

Ray Morrison spent most of his childhood in Brooklyn, New York, and Washington, D.C., but headed south after college to earn his degree in veterinary medicine and hasn't looked north since. He has happily settled in Winston-Salem, North Carolina, with his wife and three children where, when he is not writing short stories, he ministers to the needs of dogs, cats and rodents. His debut collection of short stories, *In a World of Small Truths* (Press 53), was released in November, 2012. His fiction has appeared in numerous journals, including *Ecotone*, *Carve Magazine*, *Fiction Southeast*, and *storySouth*.